Max hadn't changed seen him.

His dark wavy hair had a little more silver at the temples. It didn't make him look older, just more distinguished. What hadn't changed were those deep blue eyes that twinkled with mischief as if he saw humor in everything. The laugh lines might be a little deeper, but they only added to his charisma. She shuddered to think how ridiculous he must think her after what happened between them. The shame almost swamped her.

Max grinned.

That crooked smile on his full lips shot a stream of warmth through her despite her best effort to resist it. Lily clenched her jaw, determined she wouldn't let on to what seeing him again did to her. Thank goodness he'd only be in town for a short time.

Thank goodness.

Dear Reader,

I enjoyed writing Lily and Max's love story. The setting of Miami was something I'd never written about before, and it really added to the story. The culture of living in a metropolitan city that revolves around the beach, water, boats and hot weather had its appeal for me. I hope it does for you as well.

I did a little something different with this story as well by adding a mentally challenged sibling. Caring for a family member with a disability can be challenging at times. I know this well because I have an adult son with a mental disability. Lily has some learning to do where her sister is concerned, and Max helps show her the way.

I love to hear from my readers. Contact me at www.susancarlisle.com.

Happy reading,

Susan

FROM FLORIDA FLING TO FOREVER

SUSAN CARLISLE

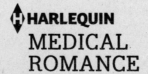

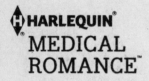

HARLEQUIN®
MEDICAL
ROMANCE™

Recycling programs
for this product may
not exist in your area.

ISBN-13: 978-1-335-40903-4

From Florida Fling to Forever

Copyright © 2021 by Susan Carlisle

This edition published by arrangement with Harlequin Books S.A.

For questions and comments about the quality of this book,
please contact us at CustomerService@Harlequin.com.

Harlequin Enterprises ULC
22 Adelaide St. West, 41st Floor
Toronto, Ontario M5H 4E3, Canada
www.Harlequin.com

Printed in U.S.A.

Susan Carlisle's love affair with books began when she made a bad grade in mathematics. Not allowed to watch TV until the grade had improved, she filled her time with books. Turning her love of reading into a love for writing romance, she pens hot medicals. She loves castles, traveling, afternoon tea, reading voraciously and hearing from her readers. Join her newsletter at susancarlisle.com.

Books by Susan Carlisle

Harlequin Medical Romance

Miracles in the Making
The Neonatal Doc's Baby Surprise

First Response
Firefighter's Unexpected Fling

Pups that Make Miracles
Highland Doc's Christmas Rescue

The Sheikh Doc's Marriage Bargain
Pacific Paradise, Second Chance
The Single Dad's Holiday Wish
Reunited with Her Daredevil Doc
Taming the Hot-Shot Doc

Visit the Author Profile page
at Harlequin.com for more titles.

To Michelle
You were always the nurse angel we needed.

CHAPTER ONE

"YOU WANT TO place the Skintec so that it just covers the incision joint but doesn't overlap the vessel more than necessary." Dr. Lily Evans demonstrated for those standing around the operating room table. She handed the tissue forceps back to her assistant and took the tiny brush filled with liquid. Using another set of tissue forceps, the fellow, the doctor who was finishing his advance training, who stood across from her folded back the corner of the patch. Lily applied the glue before the fellow laid the Skintec into place again. She continued around the square until it was secured.

The microphone of the OR observation room clicked on. A deep male voice filled the room. "If you also brush along the edges from the top, it'll give it a more firmly fixed seal."

Lily's breath caught. Her hand stilled. She knew that voice. It may have been fifteen months since she'd heard it, but she remembered the warm tone too clearly. Dr. Maxwell James. His voice had been the same one that had whispered in her ear as he kissed along her bare shoulder, up her neck, to find her lips.

She shuddered, heat washing through her. Max still had that effect on her after all this time. With heart beating faster, Lily raised her head to view the observation room with its large window. She swallowed hard. Max stood tall in a well-fitting dark suit with his white shirt open at the neck, in front of the two other people sitting there. With a hand stuffed in his left pocket, his body language screamed devil-may-care as he looked down at her.

His brilliant blue gaze met hers. She remembered it well. It appeared in her dreams often to haunt her. The man had intrigued her from the first moment she saw him years earlier at a medical conference. The problem was he had that effect on most women. Therefore, she'd always kept her distance. She wanted a special someone she could trust, that would be there for her for the long haul, a soulmate, not just a conference fling. Max was known as the playboy of the liver-transplant-surgeon conferences and that type of man didn't fit her life plan. Despite the one night she slipped up...

The corner of Max's mouth quirked upward. Lily had hoped never to face him again.

Mentally, she shook herself. Her patient waited. She had a transplant procedure to finish. Closing her mind to Max and that night when she'd lost control and humiliated herself beyond belief, she calmed her shaking hand and returned to her surgery. The transplant on this teenager would be completed to the best of her ability. Despite her desire to show her defiance and disregard Max's suggestion about the glue, she did as he said and brushed the edges. After all, he had developed the adhesive.

They may not have meshed in their personal lives, but their work had done so. She'd developed Skintec and he'd created Vseal, which together had revolutionized reattachment of vessels during a transplant. In honor of that, they were being recognized with Medical Invention of the Year Awards in the area of renal surgery. That must be why he was in town. But why so early? The ceremony was ten days away.

Lily wanted to groan. Ironically, her most significant professional achievement would forever be linked to the one man with whom she'd completely degraded herself. All because of her ex-boyfriend turned jerk, Jeff, who had picked that week to dump her. A coldness still flowed through her when she thought of that time. Now she just hoped Max didn't drag up what had happened between them and ruin her joy over her achievement.

She shook off those shameful memories and refocused on what she needed to do. "We should be able to reinfuse the liver now. Let's check for any bleeding and get this patient out to ICU." Lily removed a clamp.

The students standing around the table refocused their attention on her.

Lily watched the vessel-reconnection point carefully for bleeding. "With this new process, it has cut down on bleeding by 90 percent." Her intervention had done so by 50 percent, but paired with Max's, it had become even more effective.

She would put Dr. Max James out of her mind and get this patient closed. Maybe she'd see him only today and then not again until the awards ceremony. The least interaction she had with him the better.

An hour later, Lily spoke with the family of her patient, telling them the transplant had gone well and the liver was already working. "But," she reminded them, "the next forty-eight hours are critical. If Taylor does well during those, I fully expect him to live a long life."

The boy's mother wrapped Lily into a full hug. "Thank you, Dr. Evans."

This was what Lily found the most rewarding. Making a patient or their family happy. The feeling of knowing she made a difference in someone's life. "You're welcome."

A few minutes later, Lily headed toward her office. If she hurried, maybe she wouldn't have to see Max. Him just showing up had her nerves strung tight. She'd known he'd probably be coming to town at the end of the next week. By then, she would have been mentally prepared for him. Not now, not yet. There hadn't been any communication between them after their night together. Instead, he'd just appeared in her OR wearing a sexy grin.

By the time the awards ceremony came around, she'd have her act together. Be able to face him. Something she'd promised herself she'd never do again. She'd stopped going to conferences where she thought she might run into him. Instead, she'd sent a colleague or viewed the seminars online.

Her phone buzzed. Lily looked at her screen. It was Dr. Lee, head of transplant services at Miami University Hospital and Lily's boss. "Hello."

"Lily, can you come to my office for a few minutes?" Dr. Lee asked.

"I'm on my way to do rounds. Can it wait until after?" Lily had her fellows waiting, as well as patients.

"It won't take but a moment." The statement sounded casual, but Dr. Lee's firm note implied Lily didn't have a choice.

Minutes later, she entered Dr. Lee's office. A thin, tall woman with salt-and-pepper hair sat behind the desk. Max lounged in a chair across from her. As Lily stepped farther into the room, Max came to his feet and faced her. She clutched her hands in front of her until they hurt. He still caused her heart to pick up its pace, the traitorous organ.

Max stood close enough for her to really study him. He hadn't changed much since she last saw him. His dark wavy hair had a little more silver at the temples. It didn't make him look older, just more distinguished. What hadn't altered were those deep blue eyes that twinkled with mischief as if he saw humor in everything. The laugh lines might be a little deeper, but they only added to his charisma. She shuddered to think he saw her as ridiculous after what had happened between them. She'd been pitiful on so many levels. The shame almost swamped her.

He grinned.

That crooked smile on his full lips shot a stream of warmth through her, despite her best effort to resist it. Lily clinched her jaw, determined she wouldn't let on what seeing him again did to her. Thank goodness he'd be in town for only a short time. As soon as the ceremony was over he'd be on his way again.

Lily drew in a deep breath, straightening her shoulders. She could handle this. Him. Max had stepped into her world. A place she felt comfortable. One she controlled. In it, she could cope with him.

"I believe you know Dr. James," Dr. Lee said. "He's going to be in town until after the awards ceremony. He has asked if he might join the liver transplant team this week. See how we do things. I told him you'd show him around."

Lily's lips tightened. Dr. Lee wasn't asking her but telling her she'd be responsible for Max. Lily forced a smile and put more cheer in her voice than she felt. "I'll be glad to."

"Thank you, Lily." Dr. Lee's phone rang, and she picked it up. "Dr. James, I'll leave you in Dr. Evans's capable hands."

Max nodded at Dr. Lee and grinned at Lily. "Thank you. I look forward to that."

Lily's mouth thinned in aggravation at Dr. Lee's unintentional statement, which Max had turned into a sexual innuendo. There would *not* be anything personal between them again.

Max followed her out the door. In the hallway, she turned to face him. "I'll see you tomorrow. You can find me in the clinic seeing patients." She pointed to the left.

"Aren't you on the way to do rounds now?" Max moved up beside her.

"Yes. And I'm late." She turned away from him, being as dismissive as possible.

He matched her steps as she walked away. "Then, I'll just tag along with you, if that's okay?"

She looked back at Dr. Lee's door. Why must Max be so insistent? He'd made it clear to her at the conference he didn't really care for her company. So why the interest now? "Sure."

Max kept pace beside Lily down the wide, glossy hallway. She acted as if she wanted to get rid of him. He hadn't expected her to jump into his arms when they met again, but he'd at least thought he'd get a friendly reception. Ice-cold would be more like what he was receiving. But why? "It's nice to see you again, Lily."

She jerked to a halt and glared at him. If she used that look on her fellows, he had no doubt they toed the line. "Look, I'm sorry about that night. I made a fool of myself. What went on between us shouldn't have happened." Her gaze dropped to the floor. "I was upset and drank too much." She shook her head. "I never drink too much. That wasn't like me, and I shouldn't have come on to you. I never do that. It was unprofessional. Can we just forget it and move on?"

He stepped back and put up his hands, palms toward her. "Hey, hey. I didn't mean to bring on a tirade. I was just making polite conversation. Saying hi."

A stricken expression came over Lily's face, making him want to give her a big reassuring hug. Was that night they'd spent—almost spent—together really still that raw for her? He gave her a coaxing smile. "Let's start over. Can we do that?"

Lily looked at him with her glossy green eyes.

Seeing him again had really upset her. That hurt. More than it should have. Their time with each other hadn't ended as he would've liked but he had no wish for her to react with tears to seeing him. When she didn't say anything he dared, "You did good work in the OR today."

"Thanks," she muttered and continued down the hall.

He joined her. "I'm sorry if I stepped on your toes by suggesting how my glue should be used."

"No worries. I want what's best for my patients." She pushed the door to the stairwell open and started to climb.

Finally, her voice had evened out once more. He wanted to keep it that way. "I couldn't agree with you more. By the way, congratulations on your medical invention award."

Her shoulders relaxed. "You too."

If he kept their discussions on medicine, Lily acted as if she could handle it. When the talk became personal, she started becoming undone. Was she really that sensitive?

As they climbed the stairs, Max took a second to appreciate the woman in front of him. Ever since he saw her at a conference five years earlier, he'd been attracted to her. There hadn't been a chance to really get to know her until their last conference together, and it hadn't gone as he had hoped. Apparently, she didn't have the best of memories about it either.

He'd never thought he had a chance with the soft-spoken, so serious-looking Lily, until she came on to him that last evening of the conference. Unfortunately, that ended with her passing out in her hotel room and him receiving an emergency call and having to leave. Since then, she'd not been at another conference he had attended. Then, of all things, he'd learned they were both receiving an award for a medical invention. When his father had asked him to approach Lily about allowing The James Company to package their products together,

Max had viewed it as an opportunity to get to know Lily better.

"Kind of ironic that we're both getting the same recognition in the same year."

She glanced back at him as she made a turn to take another flight of stairs. "That's not what I'd call it."

Before Max could question her further, Lily opened the floor door and stepped through it. Ahead of them were three people wearing white lab coats, standing in a group in the hallway. They all faced her and smiled. Had his fellows ever smiled when he joined them?

Lily waved a hand toward him dismissively and started for the nearest patient door. "Hey, everyone. This is Dr. Max James. He'll be joining us today,"

Max didn't miss the look of surprise on the faces of the two men and one woman when his name was mentioned.

"Sara, how's Mr. Truman doing today?" Lily asked in an all-business tone.

"Recovering. His output is normal. His numbers on his blood work are within the normal range, and he's able to walk the hall unassisted."

Lily nodded as she looked at her computer pad. She knocked on the door and paused. At "come in," she entered. "Hello, Mr. Truman. I heard you're our star patient."

The older man grinned from the chair he sat in.

"Dr. Locke, would you like to tell Mr. Truman the good news?" Lily looked at the fellow she'd called Sara.

The doctor nodded and said to the patient, "You'll be going home tomorrow morning."

The man smiled. "Thank you. My wife will be glad to hear that."

Lily placed her hand on his shoulder. "I'll see you in my office in six weeks. No dancing until then."

Mr. Truman grinned. "I'll save that until the wedding. My daughter won't thank you for her sore toes."

Lily laughed. Max liked the sweet melody of the sound.

"I can't help with that." Lily said. "I'm a surgeon, not a dance instructor. And for that, you should be grateful. I'm an awful dancer. Dr. Locke will get you discharged. See you soon."

Their group moved out into the hall. They strolled to the next room, which was located down a few doors. Lily led them through the same process, except this time a different fellow was responsible for the patient. They all stood around the bed as Lily examined her.

"You should be getting out of here in a few more days. You're doing very well," Lily reassured her.

At the next stop, Lily's expression changed to one of concern. She looked to the fellow who hadn't had a patient yet. "How's Mr. Roth doing today?"

The fellow glanced down at his notes, but Max had the impression he knew exactly how the man was doing, without looking at them. The fellow shifted through his papers. "He's still running a low-grade fever, with no presenting reason to be doing so. He's had a CT scan, X-ray and a battery of blood work."

Lily looked at each fellow. "Any ideas about what should be done?"

"I think a MRI should be ordered," one fellow suggested.

Lily nodded and waited.

"I'd consider a biopsy," another fellow offered.

"I agree," the last one said.

"All good suggestions, but first, I'd like to examine Mr. Roth before we decide." Lily pulled her stethoscope out of her pocket.

Minutes later, Max along with the fellows were all standing beside Mr. Roth's bedside, watching Lily.

She listened to Mr. Roth's heart rate and respirations. Lily straightened and stepped back from the bed, then studied his chart. "I see you're still running a fever. Do you ache anywhere?"

"Nope." The man shook his head.

"Mr. Roth, I'm Dr. James. I'm working with Dr. Evans. Do you mind if I have a look at your incision site?" Max asked.

Lily's look met his. She hesitated a moment before she spoke to Mr. Roth. "Dr. James is visiting us from New York. He's a liver transplant surgeon, as well. Would it be okay for him to examine you?"

"I don't care who looks at me. I just want to feel better," the middle-aged man ground out.

Lily patted Mr. Roth on the arm. "We'll figure this out."

Max stepped closer. Mr. Roth pulled up his hospital gown so that his middle showed, with its large, V-shape incision. There were no obvious, outward indications of infection, such as redness or swelling. "I'm going to look at your incision site. And touch around it. Let me know if you feel any pain." Max pulled the hospital gown up farther. The incision site looked like it had healed well. He gently pushed on the skin around the scar. He could clearly feel the edge of the liver. All seemed as it should.

"Mr. Roth, would you mind rolling to your right?" The man did so, and Max applied pressure to the lower back but got no reaction from the man. "Now to the left." The man rolled and Max repeated his examination. "Thank you, Mr. Roth. You can rest back again."

Lily spoke to her patient. "We'll see that you get to feeling better soon. Try to rest."

One of the fellows pulled the door closed behind them as the group returned to the hall.

"May I see the blood work?" Max asked the fellow. "How far out from transplant is the patient?"

"Eight weeks," Lily answered.

The fellow handed him the computer pad. "Looking at his white blood count, there's no reason to believe he has an infection. I'd suggest lowering the antirejection meds and changing the IV antibiotic to a stronger one. Get a CBC again in twelve hours. I've had success doing that with cases like this."

The group looked at him. He returned the pad.

Lily paused for a moment, then nodded. "Sounds like a sound plan. We can reevaluate over the next two days. Before we consider something more invasive." To the fellow responsible for Mr. Roth, she said, "See it's done right away."

Max watched Lily. "I think you'll notice a difference quickly."

She nodded. "I hope so."

Over the next half hour, Max stayed with the group as they finished their rounds. Max couldn't help but be impressed with how quickly the transplant patients were recovering. Lily ran a good program. Maybe it stemmed from the positive rapport she had with her patients and the staff. Hers made him want to improve on his.

Finished seeing the last patient, the fellows left him and Lily.

She faced him. "Thank you for your help back there with Mr. Roth. We were running out of ideas."

"I hope mine works." Max couldn't deny he liked having Lily's praise, despite it being unexpected.

For once, she met his look with a direct one of her own. "Do you really plan to spend all your time in Miami in a hospital?"

"Not all the time, but I wanted to see how your program works. See if there's something I can take home to mine in New York City."

She started down the hall toward the stairwell door. "I'm sure following me around must be dull. Wouldn't you rather go to the beach?"

Max liked she'd become comfortable enough

with him to ask a personal question. He grinned. "Is that an invitation?"

Lily stopped and gave him a piercing no-nonsense look. "No."

"Come on. I think we could find some time to spend on the beach." Max gave her a teasing smile.

She opened her mouth to speak, but he raised a hand. "I know. You have clinic tomorrow."

"Yeah, and it's held in the building next door. Just ask the receptionist at the front desk and she can tell you where to find me."

"I'll see you then." Max lifted a hand and walked to the bank of elevators.

The next morning, Lily entered the building to find Max leaning casually against the front desk, talking to the woman behind it. She looked pleased to have such a handsome man's attention. Lily even heard a giggle. Max hadn't changed.

Even before they had gotten together that dreadful night, Lily had heard the talk about Max being a big flirt with little substance. Lily was looking for someone who would be her partner through life, not someone looking for nothing but a good time. She'd watched him from afar at conferences for years. No different than most women, she'd been drawn to him like the proverbial moth to the flame. Max just had something about him that interested her. With his easygoing personality, he had a way with people, especially women. She fallen for his charm, despite knowing better. Weak, she'd just been weak.

"Good morning," he drawled and handed her a cup. "It's tea. I didn't figure you for the coffee type."

Max had already placed her in a *type* pool? She wasn't sure how she felt about that. Taking the paper cup with the cap on it, she said, "Thanks."

He shrugged. "No problem. So, is there any special case you're seeing today?"

"Most are post-op patients." Lily headed down the hallway toward the wing of the building where she saw them. "But I do have one that's coming in that might interest you."

"Good morning, Dr. Evans," the nurse standing in the hall said. "Your first patient is waiting in room one."

"Thanks, Carol." Leaving the tea on a corner of a counter, Lily took the electronic tablet from the nurse.

Disappointed to leave his hot coffee behind, Max did the same and hurried after Lily.

Going to the closest door, she knocked and

entered. "Hello, Mrs. Sandoz. How're you feeling?"

The middle-aged woman, her black hair liberally streaked with white, smiled. "I feel much better than I did before the transplant."

"Thank you so much, Dr. Evans. It's so nice to have my wife back," Mr. Sandoz said.

"I'm glad to hear it. Mr. and Mrs. Sandoz, this is Dr. James. He's visiting with us this week."

Max gave Mrs. Sandoz one of his charming smiles. The woman's eyes warmed, and she returned it. Was there no end to Max's appeal to women?

Lily scrolled through Mrs. Sandoz's chart on the pad, then took the chair next to her. "May I give you a listen? Your X-rays look great." Lily pulled her stethoscope out of the pocket of her white lab coat.

Max took the pad from her and brushed the screen, looking at Mrs. Sandoz's chart as Lily listened to the woman's heartbeats and respirations.

Lily stood. "Now, if you'll lie down on the exam table, I'd like to look at your incision site."

Mrs. Sandoz went to the table.

Max stepped up and offered his hand to the

older woman. "Here, take my hand and I'll help you lie back."

"Thank you." The woman placed her hand in his and the other on his forearm, steadying herself as she stepped up and sat on the table.

Lily couldn't help but soften toward Max for his consideration for the older woman.

Placing a hand at her back, he gently supported Mrs. Sandoz as she eased back. "I've seen enough of my patients struggle to lower themselves after surgery to know it isn't always comfortable."

Mrs. Sandoz settled on the table. She pulled her full blouse up beneath her breast, revealing the large pink incision that went from one side of her body to the other.

Lily studied the area. "It all looks good. You're healing well."

"It still feels tight when I move." She brushed her hand over the area.

"It'll take a while for things to get back to normal. But overall, you're doing great. You can start driving again. I'd like to see you back here in three months. Don't forget to have your lab work done."

Mrs. Sandoz pulled her shirt down. Lily helped the woman sit up.

"Thank you, Dr. Evans," Mrs. Sandoz said with a large grin.

"You're welcome. See you soon." Lily smiled over her shoulder as she opened the door.

Max followed Lily out into the hall. "She looks great. I read in the surgery notes you used my glue on her."

Lily rolled her eyes. He would pick that out of the record. "Yes, Vseal does work."

He grinned. "It's always nice to hear admiration from such an esteemed surgeon."

Lily huffed and walked to the next examination room.

CHAPTER TWO

MAX COULDN'T DENY the more he was around Lily, the more impressed he was with her and her transplant program. Spending the morning shadowing her only confirmed what he'd heard and read. She was a consummate, caring professional. That being the case, maybe she would agree to his proposal. If they were to package Vseal and Skintec together, they could make a lot of money and help his father's company in the process. This was Max's chance to impress his father for once. He'd been a disappointment for so long, but if he could pull this deal together with Lily, maybe his father's view would change. Alone, his and Lily's products were good, but together, they were outstanding. The James Company could move up the ranks of medical manufacturing if he could work this out with Lily. Would she consider his suggestion?

Even after spending some time in the last

twenty-four hours together, Lily remained cool toward him. Why, he couldn't figure out. Nothing had happened that night. He didn't take advantage of drunk women. When he'd seen her sitting alone at the table by the pool, drinking, his protective side had won out. He had to admit he'd been tempted to stay after she invited him to her room, but one of the many things his father had insisted Max be was a gentleman. And only in one area had he gone against his father's wishes, and being a gentleman hadn't been it.

"So, what now?" he asked as they walked back to the clinic's nurses' desk. "Lunch, I hope. I'll buy."

"You don't need to do that. I have to go over to the hospital and check on a patient." Lily handed the charting pad to the nurse and smiled.

Max wished she'd offer him one of those smiles, at least once. They were going to have to get what had happened between them—or hadn't—aired out. "How about lunch, then I'll go with you to see Mr. Roth?"

She studied him for a long moment then sighed. "Okay."

Max smiled at the nurse. "It was nice to meet you." He turned back to Lily. "Have you seen Mr. Roth's morning lab tests yet?"

Lily started down the hall toward the front of the building. "I have. They look better. But I'd like to see him myself."

"After lunch. I'm starving."

"I usually eat in my office or skip it." She sounded as if he'd invited her to a funeral.

"I don't like to eat by myself. Join me. I don't even know where the cafeteria is. And you're supposed to be taking care of me." He grinned at her like a cartoon character.

She huffed and walked ahead of him. They continued through the building, took the outside door and started across a garden area with a softly bubbling fountain, a brick walk and palm foliage all around.

"It feels so good here." Max looked up at the sky. "I could get used to all this warmth and sunshine."

Lily chuckled. "You think that, until it's blistering hot in the middle of the summer."

"I'd like to try it at least once." While they had a few moments together, he intended to straighten things out between them. If he didn't, he'd never get her to agree to a partnership. There was too much at stake for them not to at least trust each other. "I haven't seen you at a conference in the last few months."

"I watched them online. I've been too busy

to get away." There was a hard, sad note in her voice.

"I've looked for you."

She glanced at him but didn't slow her pace. "Why? So you could humiliate me again?"

He touched her elbow. "Why would you say that?"

Lily gave him a pointed look and stepped away from his touch.

That hurt for some odd reason. "I think we need to talk. Come over here." He pointed in the direction of a bench secluded in the greenery, where they wouldn't be overheard or disturbed. "Please."

"I thought you were hungry." She looked toward the door as if she were a mouse preparing to escape a trap.

"I think it can wait five minutes. The way you've been gigging me, my guess is you'll never have time. I'm going to be here for a week, and I don't want a misunderstanding standing between us the entire time. Please."

Lily shielded her face from the sun with a hand as she watched him. "I don't have time to talk about this right now." She shook her head. "Anyway, I just want to forget it."

He met her gaze. "My feelings would be hurt if you did forget. I haven't."

Lily's lips pursed as she gave him an exasperated look. "There's nothing to talk about. I understand completely. I was the one who woke up alone. I was your conference good time!"

A nurse exited the hospital and gave them a curious look. Max stepped toward the quiet spot, and Lily followed. "Listen, nothing happened between us other than I took a tipsy woman to her room and put her to bed. Call me decimating, but I don't have sex with women who won't remember it."

Her eyes widened. "What? We didn't…?"

Max shook his head. "No, we didn't. Not that I wouldn't have enjoyed it, but like I said, the time wasn't right."

"But I remember you undressing me. Kissing me," she said so softly that he had to lean close to hear.

He kept his voice low. "I did. Then, the next thing I knew, you were curled up in the middle of the bed asleep." He grinned. "Snoring, I believe."

She gasped, turning her back to him. "I didn't!"

"Yep. You did." He felt sorry for her in her embarrassment. "I think you already had had a few when I came to sit with you by the pool, then you insisted you wanted another."

Lily hung her head. "I had. And I don't usually drink. I hate being out of control."

"That doesn't surprise me."

She glared at him. "What do you mean?"

"Just that you're a woman who likes to keep a tight hold on her world and emotions." He met her look.

She returned it without blinking. "You don't know me well enough to make those assumptions."

Max shrugged. "Maybe not. But that's not what we were discussing. That night after you passed out, I put you to bed. I didn't think you'd appreciate me going through your things to find whatever you sleep in. I'd have been there when you woke, but I had to leave. I was called in for emergency surgery. But you were already down for the count."

Lily put her head in her hands and groaned. "And to think I was humiliated before."

Max chuckled. "Hey, you shouldn't feel that way. I was flattered. I knew enough about you to know you aren't promiscuous. So, are we good now?"

Lily shrugged. "I guess. Please forgive me for being so, uh, unwelcoming to you."

"I understand. Don't worry about it." He smiled. "In that case, could we maybe start again? After all, you're the only person I know in Miami."

"I guess so." Meeting his look, she said, "I promise nothing like that'll ever happen again."

For some reason, that disappointed him. Especially since he'd thought more than once of the shapely curves and silky skin he'd seen and touched briefly that night in the hotel. Lily had interested him. She still did. "Come on. Let's have lunch and then see Mr. Roth."

Lily nodded.

He stepped ahead of her and opened the side door leading into the hospital. They went to the nearest elevator. After entering, Max watched Lily as the door closed. Her scent wrapped around him in the closed space. She smelled of sunshine, tropical flowers and a fresh rain. The women he usually dated wore the latest popular, expensive cologne. None smelled as lovely as Lily. In fact in most ways, they were nothing like Lily. Why, then, did he find her so appealing?

"You know your glue is really brilliant." Lily spoke as if trying to fill the silence between them.

"Thank you. Have you had offers to sell Skintec?"

"You know I have. Just like I'm sure you have had offers for Vseal."

Max grinned. "A few." The door opened and they stepped off the elevator. "I want to talk to you about that…"

Lily's phone buzzed and she answered it. "Hey there."

Max looked at Lily. Her entire demeanor had changed. Her voice took on a sweet note as if she were speaking to a child. "Yes, I'll be on time."

Did Lily have a significant other? In almost two years, a lot could change.

"Yes, yes we'll have tater tots and chicken strips. I know they're your favorite." She turned her back to him.

Was she talking to her child?

"I have to go now. See you soon." Lily pocketed her phone and turned to him. "The cafeteria is down this way."

"I had no idea you had a child." Too curious not to find out.

"It was my sister."

Lily looked up to see Max take a huge bite out of the hamburger he'd ordered from the cafeteria grill. "You were hungry."

"Yeah. I had to leave the hotel before they

had breakfast laid out in order to meet you on time." He continued eating.

"Where're you staying?" She watched, fascinated by the movement of his throat.

"In South Beach."

"Oh, I love those retro hotels. Which one?" She couldn't help her interest.

Using a napkin, he wiped a dot of ketchup off his chin. "Hotel Blue Sea."

"I know the one. It has the neon-blue waves along the side. Right across the street from the beach." She would love to explore the lodging.

"That's the one." He gave her a long look.

"Nice place." She'd never been inside, but she wouldn't be saying that to Max. That would be far too suggestive. She needed to change the subject. It seemed she had to do that often around him. "Are you still at New York Central Hospital?"

"I am." Maxwell picked up his cup and pulled his drink through the straw.

"You've a big program there." She pushed the lettuce of her salad around.

Max set the cup down on the table. "We do, but there still isn't as much work as I'd like."

"Our program here is almost overwhelmed. There aren't enough doctors to handle the need."

Max nodded. "That's what I've heard."

Who'd he heard that from? Had he been checking up on her? The program? Why?

He lifted his chin toward her uneaten salad. "Are you saving room for tater tots and chicken strips tonight? Interesting menu."

"It's what Ivy likes." Lily poked at a lettuce leaf again.

"Ivy? That's your sister's name?" Humor circled his words.

"Something funny?" She dared him to laugh.

"No. Just interesting. Ivy and Lily. It sounds like a garden."

Lily watched as he tried to cover his smile with the hamburger. She glared at him. "It isn't polite to make fun of people's names."

He looked around innocently. "I've not said a word about anyone's names."

Lily leaned forward as she continued to glare. "No, but I know what you're thinking."

He finished his bite. "What? That your names make me think of springtime."

"They're awful." She sat back, a grin on her lips. "Not so bad apart, but when said together, they're pretty bad."

"I wouldn't say *bad*, just ear catching." He returned her smile.

She smirked. "Thanks, that's a nice way of putting it."

"I guess Ivy lives nearby, since you were

talking about dinner together tonight." Max returned to his hamburger.

She didn't talk about Ivy much, especially to strangers. Wasn't that what Max was? "Yes."

"Do you have other siblings?" He took another bite of his burger.

"No. Only Ivy." She watched him chew and swallow. Why did Max fascinate her so?

"I'm guessing you two are close."

She shifted in her chair aware of him watching her. "Very. I'm Ivy's guardian."

"Guardian?" Surprise rang clear in his voice.

She met his look with a direct one. "My sister is mentally challenged. Has been since birth. She has been my responsibility since my parents died in a car accident five years ago."

He placed what was left of his burger on the plate and wiped his mouth. "I'm sorry to hear that. About your parents. That's tough."

Lily appreciated his sentiment, but she didn't need his pity. "It has been, but Ivy and I have adjusted."

The expression in his eyes had turned from teasing to kind. "I'm sure it hasn't been easy."

"Nothing's easy all the time. We just keep moving forward." How many times had she told herself that? Hadn't she said that when Jeff dropped her just before they were supposed to spend the week together at the fated conference? Again, after Max had left her in bed alone. After her parents died. Yeah, she'd just kept moving.

"I guess you do." Max returned to his sandwich.

"Do you have brothers and sisters?" She wasn't sure why she wanted to know more about him, but she did.

"One of both. Jessie, my sister and her family live in Atlanta. Rob and his family live in Chicago where I grew up." There was fond note in his voice as he used their names.

"Are you close?"

He nodded, a softer look coming over his face. "Yeah. We enjoy being together. I wish it was more often."

"And your parents?" She really wanted to know more about the people important to him.

"Still alive and kicking. Mom's involved in every charity in town." He made it sound more indulgent than critical.

Something about the fact he said nothing further concerning his father felt odd, especially compared to the warmth in his voice regarding his mother.

"Are you finished?" Max abruptly dropped his napkin on the tray. "I want to see Mr. Roth, then I have to go to the hotel and return some phone calls this afternoon."

"Yeah, sure." She stood and picked up her tray, heading toward the disposal area. Did his sudden urge to leave have anything to do with not wanting her to question him about his father?

With their trays put away, they walked out into the hall.

"Hey," Max said, "I like where I'm staying, but I really don't want to sit around the hotel the entire weekend. Since I'm from out of town and this is your regular stomping grounds, how about showing me around? I'd love to see some of the city."

"I can't." She shook her head. If she could, would she agree? She and Max might have moved beyond what had happened that night at the conference, but she hadn't forgotten it.

"Or won't?"

Why was he pushing her? "I promised to take my sister to the beach."

His face brightened. "My hotel has a dedicated area on the beach. Why don't you bring her there?"

Lily looked at him, her eyes wide with surprise. "Are you serious?"

He returned a frank gaze as if he thought

his invitation wasn't the least out of the norm. "Sure, why not?"

Max's look of anticipation made her say against her better judgement, "I, uh… I guess we could do that."

Max wouldn't have been shocked if Lily had texted him the next morning to say she wouldn't be coming. Yet it was time for her to arrive and he hadn't heard from her. Remaining optimistic, an hour ago, he'd reserved two cabanas. He looked toward the street again, hoping to catch sight of Lily.

Two women holding hands crossed the road. There Lily was. He walked through the soft white sand to meet her. A large-brimmed hat sat on her head, and dark glasses covered her eyes, but he recognized her walk. She wore a flowing cover-up with a pointed hem, which floated around her ankles. A small cooler was in the hand not clasping her sister's.

Ivy looked very much like Lily. The hair color, the shape of her face. Were Ivy's eyes the same? They were covered by sunglasses, as well. Despite their similarities, their demeanors were different. There was something childlike in Ivy's actions.

"Hey. I was wondering if you were going to

make it." Max pulled off his glasses and smiled briefly at Lily and longer at Ivy.

"It, uh… It, uh, took us a few minutes to find a parking place," Lily seemed to struggle to say.

Even with the glasses covering her eyes, Max had the distinct impression her focus remained on his bare chest. "I didn't think to make arrangements for your parking. Sorry. I will next time. Let me take that cooler for you."

Lily released it but not before their hands brushed. She quickly pulled hers away. "No problem. Max, I'd like you to meet my sister, Ivy. Ivy, say hello."

Ivy looked at the sand she kicked with the toe of her shoe. She said a shy "hello."

"Hi, Ivy. I'm glad you came today. Would you like me to take that bag for you?"

"No. It is mine." She pulled it tighter to her.

"Okay." Apparently, he'd have two Evans women to win over today. Why it mattered so much, he wasn't sure. "I have us some cabanas right down here." He started back toward the bright yellow umbrellas with blue waves that matched the one on the wall of the hotel. Double lounges sat beneath them. He pointed to theirs. "You may have whichever you want."

"I like this one," Ivy stated and plopped the

bag down on the cushion, then looked around. "I don't know this beach."

"I told you we were going to try a new one." Lily pulled a towel out of a bag that had been over her shoulder and spread it on the lounge next to Ivy's.

"Where are we?" Ivy asked, looking panicked.

Lily placed her hand on Ivy's arm, gaining her attention. "We're in front of Max's hotel. He wanted us to come to the beach with him today."

"Oh, this is Max's beach." Ivy peered around again in awe.

Max chuckled. "Something like that."

"I'm not used to such luxury at the beach." Lily settled on the lounge next to Ivy's and looked around.

Max dipped his head under the umbrella and sat on the lounger next to hers. "For somebody from New York City, I thought it best my skin wasn't out exposed all the time, even wearing sunscreen."

Lily laughed. "You're probably right. The sun is strong here year-round."

A ripple of heat ran through him that had nothing to do with the sun. "You need to do that more often."

"What?" Lily faced him.

"Laugh. It's a nice sound." Max watched as a pink tint traveled up her neck to her face.

"I want to go to the water," Ivy announced.

"Okay, but first you have to make sure you have on plenty of lotion. You don't want to burn." Lily sounded like a mother hen talking to her chick.

"I know. I can do it." Ivy dug into her bag.

"I was working on the same thing when you got here." Max picked up his bottle of sunscreen. "I still need some on my back. Lily, would you mind?" He offered her the bottle.

Lily looked at it as if it were a snake. Her mouth formed a circle. He could almost see the wheels turning in her mind. She slowly took the tube from him.

He presented her with his back. Lily took so long to start the job he glanced over his shoulder to see if she was still there. Her hand hovered over his right shoulder. He turned around and waited. Finally, there was a faint brush of something cool against his back. Her fingertips shook for a moment then became bolder as she smoothed the lotion around. His chest tightened while his breathing quickened. As she worked her way over his skin, his muscles rippled beneath. He experienced every movement in slow-motion detail.

Lily's fingers wrapped his shoulder, then

moved to the center of his back. Her hand left him. He held his breath until it returned. This time she rubbed one way, then the other—with purpose, as if she were trying to get the job done as soon as possible.

Too soon and not soon enough for his body's relief, she said with a shake in her voice, "Done."

Max needed to put some distance between them. If he'd had any idea he'd react like a teenager to a girl's first touch when Lily stroked her fingers over him, he'd have figured out some other way to get lotion on, or done without.

"I'm ready," Ivy announced.

Lily cleared her throat. "Go on, but wait on me before you get in the water."

"Hurry," Ivy threw over her shoulder as she headed toward the water.

Max found the interaction between the sisters interesting. Lily's mothering instinct was clearly in overdrive with Ivy. He didn't have much experience with adults with learning disabilities, so he couldn't question Lily's protective attitude. "I'll go down and join her."

A look of relief washed over Lily's face as she picked up the lotion again. "I'll be there as soon as I finish putting this on."

Max almost offered to help her but thought

better of it. He feared that once he started touching Lily, he wouldn't stop. Instead, he worked his way out from under the umbrella. "Is it okay if we go ahead and get in the water? Can Ivy swim?"

"Yes. And yes."

He started walking away.

"Thanks, Max."

Lily watched Max and Ivy as they splashed water at each other. His large shoulders glistened in the sunlight. The muscles of his back tensed and relaxed as he played and laughed with Ivy. He really was a gorgeous man. He didn't have the body of a thin young man but had one of maturity that made her think of steadfastness, security. One that could shelter.

For a few minutes earlier, she'd forgotten herself and enjoyed rubbing lotion on Max. Her attraction to him had taken over and led her down a trail of desire she'd not intended to travel. She couldn't let that happen again. He was here for only seven more days, and then he'd be gone again. Being left behind once more wasn't something she wanted any part of. She needed to find the man who she was enough for that he would stay around. Max wasn't that type. They would be friends and nothing more.

What would it hurt for her to enjoy watching him while she could?

"Let's splash Lily," Ivy yelled.

She and Max turned to Lily, who had been peacefully bobbing with the waves. "You better not gang up on me. I don't get mad. I get even."

"We're going to get you," Ivy said.

The words were hardly out of Ivy's mouth when Lily was hit in the face with a shower of water. Lily wiped it away from her eyes to see Ivy and Max grinning at her. "Now you've done it."

Over the next few minutes, they had a water fight, laughing and having a good time. Max acted as if he was in his element. Jeff had cared nothing about Ivy. In fact, the less interaction he'd had with her, the better he'd liked it. Ivy had been a bone of contention between them from the beginning. Jeff had accused Lily of thinking of Ivy more than she did him. Lily had tried to overlook his attitude in the hopes it would improve with time. Now she could see it for what it was—immature jealousy. He'd never shown Ivy the interest that Max had in just these last few minutes.

Max moved closer to her. "Ivy, I think Lily has had enough."

Lily agreed. She hadn't been on the prevailing end of the splash fest, but Ivy had enjoyed it.

Max pushed water at Ivy as he turned his head to protect his face from the water coming at him. "It's been too long since I've done this. I'd forgotten how much fun it can be."

Lily smirked. "It depends on who's on the winning side."

"My brother and sister used to always be against me." Max gave her a self-satisfied smile. "But I still always won."

"Why am I not surprised? I don't imagine you lose often." Lily pushed her wet hair out of her face.

He grinned. "Not if I can't help it."

"Did your family live near the lake?" For some reason, she was curious about Max's past. Even when she shouldn't be.

"No, but my mother made sure we went to the beach for a week every year." He looked off toward the horizon.

Was there a sadness there? "Your father didn't go?"

"He didn't have time. Too busy building the business." A bitterness surrounded the words.

"What does your daddy do?"

"He's the head of The James Company." Max continued to look into the distance.

Lily's eyes widened. "I know that name.

That's one of the largest medical supply companies in the world. They want me to sign a contract with them."

"Yeah."

"I hadn't put your name and the company together." Lily couldn't get over Max being the son of one of the most well-to-do men in that industry.

Max moved toward Ivy. "Hey, Ivy, do you want to see if we can see some fish?"

Max had certainly put an end to that conversation. The James Company was a huge outfit. They manufactured all types of equipment. She'd read the name on her surgical instruments, even had a contact number for them.

They stayed in the water for a while longer before Max said, "I don't know about you ladies, but I could use something to eat."

"We brought some snacks." Lily started toward the shore.

Max joined her. "I need something more substantial after that water battle, don't you, Ivy? How about pizza?"

Lily couldn't help but admire his gorgeous physique of broad shoulders, thick muscles, sleek skin that tapered to trim hips as Max moved ahead of her through the waist-deep water.

"I love pizza," Ivy squealed.

Max grinned over his shoulder, a grin that came close to taking Lily's breath away. "I thought you might. I was told a pizza truck parks only a couple of blocks away. I was going to walk down there and get us a pie."

"Can I go with you?" Ivy asked.

Max stepped out of the water. "Sure you can. We'll let Lily stay here and lie in the sun, and we'll deliver."

"Max—" Lily moved toward him.

His eyes narrowed as he gave her a meaningful look before his voice turned soft. "I've got this."

Lily pushed her nervous concern down. "Ivy, you stay close to Max. Do as he says."

"I will." Ivy happily pranced off beside Max.

Lily stood there in wonder before she mentally shook herself and followed them out of the water.

They gathered around the lounges.

"You need your cover-up on, Ivy." Lily picked up a towel to dry off.

"I know," she said in a sharp tone.

"Will you hand me the T-shirt on that bag between the chairs?" Max asked Lily.

She picked the garment off the top of the carryall. As she handed it to him, the rich scent that was Max's fluttered beneath her nose. She stopped herself just short of bringing it up to her face and inhaling.

Ivy had her cover-up on. "Let's go."

"We shouldn't be long." Max leaned closer to Lily. "By the way, you look gorgeous in a swimsuit."

Lily's breath caught as heat shot through her. She watched as Max's strong legs with thick thighs carried him through the sand while Ivy chatted happily beside him. What Lily intended not to let occur was happening. Her attraction to Max was growing.

Settling on the lounge, Lily closed her eyes, enjoying the warmth and a few moments when nothing was required of her. They were rare between work, Ivy and her research. Slowly, she drifted off to sleep with thoughts of rubbing her hands across Max's shoulders.

She woke to Ivy lying on the lounger to her left and Max stretched out on the one to her right. His head rested on his hands, clasped behind his head.

"I wondered how long you'd sleep."

Max's low rumble rippled through her. She jerked her head around to look at him. "How did you know I was awake?"

"Um, a good guess?" Humor filled his voice.

"You've been watching me?" She raised her

sunglasses to glare at him before letting them drop into place again.

"I don't remember you being so sensitive." He sat up, turning to face her, giving her a clear view of his chest. Grateful for her dark glasses, she took full advantage of the vista in front of her.

"You remember something about me?"

"I remember a lot about you. I've paid attention to you at conferences and followed your career for years."

Lily wasn't sure what to make of that. Somehow it made her sit straighter.

Some time passed before he said, "I like the name Lily. It's soft and sweet-sounding like you."

"My name might imply that, but I assure you I don't fit your definition."

Max chuckled. "I don't think that's true. I've seen you with your patients. With Ivy. The only person I know of who you don't have a soft spot for is me."

Little did he know. "We agreed there would be nothing between us."

"If I remember correctly, it was you who said something like that." He shifted on the lounge, resting his knee against her chair.

"I did."

He shook his head. "But I made no such statement."

"Max don't start."

"Okay, okay. We'll keep it a happy family day."

She glanced at Ivy, who softly snored beside her. "That's what it should be."

"You hungry? We left you some pizza. It's not hot, but it shouldn't be too bad. If you'd rather, I can order something from the hotel."

Why must he be so considerate? It made it hard not to like him. "Pizza is fine."

Max picked up a paper plate with a napkin over it. "Your drink is right here." He pointed to a soft drink can in a cup holder beside him. "Ivy told me what you like."

Lily grinned as she took the plate from him. "I bet she did. She likes to be the one who has the answers."

"She's a sweet girl."

"She is." Lily took a bite of her pizza.

"Does she live with you?"

Lily picked up her drink and took a swallow. "No. She lives and works in a group home about thirty minutes from here."

"I figured you must have some help, otherwise it would be hard for you to work."

"Sometimes it still is, but I've managed."

She replaced her drink, making sure she didn't touch Max's leg in the process.

He placed his elbows on his knees, leaning in closer. "You're a good sister, Lily."

Max watched Lily's body relax. She had appreciated his compliment. He could only imagine how difficult it had been to realize she would be responsible for her sister for the rest of her life. That had to have been life changing.

"I'm hot. I think I'll get back in the water," Ivy said.

Lily looked at Ivy. He silently watched them.

"Sure. I feel like a swim too." Lily stuffed her half-eaten pizza into an empty plastic bag she pulled out of her carrier. Without a backward look at him, she pulled off her cover-up. His chest tightened as her feminine curves came into full view. Her beautifully rounded breasts that he remembered from months ago still temped him.

Before Max knew what had happened, Lily and Ivy were leaving.

Ivy said, "Are you coming, Max?"

Lily took her hand. "Max may want to take a nap. We can swim without him."

Ivy looked perplexed as she glanced back over her shoulder while Lily tugged her away. Max took his time joining them. They were treading water and laughing as waves slapped against them.

"Hey, Max." Ivy waved.

"Hi, Ivy. You look like you're having fun."

"We are. Lily and I like the waves."

Max looked at Lily and grinned. With her hat pulled low and her sunglasses on, he couldn't read her reaction.

"Ivy, watch for the waves. You don't want one to knock you over." The words were hardly out of Lily's mouth when a wall of water struck her and carried her under.

Her body hit his. Max reached for her. His hands went to her waist as he struggled to remain standing. He pulled her back against him, but the sand shifted under his feet and they fell backward. Lily twisted to right herself before the next wave hit them, while he worked to stand. Her hands ran over his chest, finding his shoulders. His hands tightened on her waist and supported her as she stood.

Lily's hat drooped and her glasses sat askew as she stammered, "I'm sorry. I didn't mean to knock you down. The wave…"

His thumbs brushed over her waist. "Hey, I'm not complaining. I like it when a beautiful woman grabs me."

"I didn't—"

He grinned. "That's not how I remember it."

"Ivy!" Lily turned.

Max let his hands fall away. "She's fine. She fared better than you."

"That wave got you good." Ivy laughed. "Better than when Max and I splashed you."

Lily pushed away from him.

He was tempted to pull her back.

Lily moved toward Ivy. "Yeah, it did. We need to think about going."

"Do we have to?" Ivy whined.

"Yeah, it's getting late." Lily started toward the shore.

Max hated to see her leave. He'd had a good day, something he couldn't recall happening in a long time. What would Lily say if he begged them to stay longer? Too soon they were walking toward the loungers.

Ivy had moved ahead of Lily and him. "I know that today was family day. Do you have plans with Ivy tomorrow night?"

"No, I'll take her home tomorrow afternoon."

He touched her arm. She stopped and turned to him. "Then, how about having dinner with me? I have something I'd like to discuss with you."

"We can't do that now?"

He looked at the crowd on the beach. "It's related to our innovations, and I'd prefer we aren't interrupted when we discuss what I have in mind. Why don't we have dinner here at the hotel restaurant, where it'll be less public?"

"I don't know..."

He grinned. "Come on, Lily. You can trust me. I thought I'd proved that."

She sighed. "All right."

"I'll pick you up at eight."

Lily started walking again. "No, I'll meet you in the lobby at eight."

CHAPTER THREE

LILY ADMIRED THE retro waterfall-chandelier's light reflecting off the black-and-white tiled lobby floor of Max's hotel. Orange sofas and yellow chairs and ocean-blue pillows with the signature wave imprinted on them were arranged in groups around the large space. A reception desk constructed of clear glass blocks with a wood top, creating a curve, was located to the right side of the entrance doors. On the walls were black-and-white pictures of beach days from the 1950s. The hotel was all Lily thought it would be and more.

As she walked farther inside, Max rose to his feet from where he had been sitting in one of the chairs. He looked as if he belonged there, attired in a white button-down dress shirt, cream-colored jacket and navy slacks. Everything about him screamed suave male.

The grin on his lips appeared sincere and made her middle flutter. How could she resist him? Despite their understanding about their failed night together, she remained unsure about him. She had a sense there was more to his interest in her than he'd let on so far. Maybe she'd find out if she was right tonight.

He stopped in front of her. "Hi, Lily. I'm glad you came."

"I said I would."

"You did. The restaurant is this way." Max's fingers touched her elbow long enough to direct her toward the elevators.

When the doors opened, Max's hand came to rest on the small of her back as they entered, then it fell away. Another couple joined them in the small space just as the doors closed, crowding her against Max. She could feel his heat along her back. The old elevator jerked as it started up. She stepped back to steady herself. Max's hand found her waist again and remained there. The evening had already turned into more than she had prepared for emotionally.

To her relief and disappointment, the warmth went away after they stepped out of the elevator onto the hotel rooftop. An attractive young woman stood beside a slick podium. "Hello, Dr. James. We have your table ready for you."

The area was like a tropical oasis, with palm trees and foliage set so that they created small alcoves with tables neatly tucked between them. Blue, pink and white lights were laced under and around the greenery and fixtures. A small candle with a frosted globe glowed in the center of each table. It reminded her of a nightclub she'd seen only in movies.

Max held her chair while she settled in at the two-person table in the corner where they could look out at the ocean. She'd never been to a more romantic spot. Wasn't this a business meeting?

Max took his chair. "I hope this all suits you."

Lily couldn't picture anywhere that she would've liked more. A trio played softly in the distance. She looked around, then back at him. "Are you kidding? This is the most amazing place I've ever been."

"I'm glad I get to share your first time here with you. I would've thought you'd come to a restaurant like this regularly."

"I work most of the time, and when I'm not doing that, I'm with Ivy." What she didn't say was that she watched her finances closely because she carried a content fear that if something happened to her there wouldn't be enough money to care for Ivy.

"You haven't been on dates to places like this?" His look didn't waver from her.

"My ex didn't like going anywhere fancy. He was more of a pizza-and-TV kind of guy."

Max's brow rose. "Your ex? Husband? You've not mentioned him before."

"Ex-boyfriend. It was a long time ago. In fact, we broke up the night before I came to that fated conference."

Max pursed his lips and nodded his head thoughtfully. "So that's why you were drinking by yourself and had a sudden interest in me."

The gentle breeze off the ocean rustled the palms around them, cooling her heated cheeks. "Yeah. I wasn't in a good place."

"Why's that?" He wanted to know, to understand her. For a minute there, he wasn't sure she would answer him.

Finally she said, "For weeks, Jeff and I had talked about him coming with me to the conference. It was supposed to be a shared vacation. He didn't care for Ivy going places with us, so it was to be our time away. The night before we were to leave, he dumped me because he said I wasn't worth taking on all my baggage, which meant Ivy. But he also didn't like that I wouldn't give him an answer about Skintec. See, he was a salesman for a biotech company. He wanted me to give them the rights to my invention, with him a leader of the project. I told him I wasn't ready to do that. I wanted to have my lawyer look at contracts first. Jeff didn't like that. He said the only reason he'd been interested in me in the first place was to get a chance at Skintec.

"Things blew up. There I was, stupidly thinking he was going to ask me to marry him while we were away." Lily shook her head. "I'm sorry. You didn't need to hear all that."

"I don't mind, and it sounded like you needed to say it."

She appreciated his tone of compassion. "I hate to admit it, but what Jeff did still stings. Worse, it made me act like a fool in front of you and others who I value their respect. I never do that sort of thing. I'm so ashamed."

Max smiled a smile that reassured her. "We all have people who make us say and do things we wouldn't otherwise."

A waiter came to stand at their table.

"What would you like to drink?" Max asked.

"Something fruity. With an umbrella."

Max chuckled and told the young man, "Make that two."

Lily studied him for a moment. "You don't strike me as a fruit-drinking man."

"Normally, I'm not, but it sounded kind of fun."

She looked out toward the ocean. "You like to have a good time."

"I do. I think life is too short to take it too seriously. My job is serious enough for me."

She wished she had the pleasure of not seeing life so seriously, but that wasn't the case.

"It gets hot in this part of the country in the summertime, but I do love living near the ocean. Tell me why you picked this particular hotel to stay in?"

"My father stays here when he comes to Miami. He recommended it."

She picked up her drink. That's the father he didn't talk about yesterday when he spoke about his family.

Max fingered the candle shade. "Did Ivy have a good time at the beach?"

"You know she did. She thinks you are the best thing since sliced bread. As usual, you have a way with women."

His expression turned thoughtful. "That would be with every woman but you."

He affected her. Too much so. She couldn't afford to show it.

"At the risk of making you angry, I want to apologize again for what happened at the conference."

"I might have overreacted." Of that, she was sure. But she still had a hard time working past her embarrassment.

"It's okay. I understand."

"I doubt you really do." What would a man like him know about his pride being damaged? Who wouldn't be pleased with him?

"Why do you say that?"

"I can't imagine that a woman has ever managed to humiliate you."

"Humiliate me? Maybe not." His look remained fixed on her. "Disturb me, concern me. Stay in my thoughts. Yeah."

Was he talking about her?

"I think you're a very special person, Lily. Especially where your sister is concerned."

She twisted her fingers around each other in her lap. It made her nervous to have Max's complete attention. "I appreciate that. Few people understand the challenges of what it's like to be responsible for a mentally challenged adult."

He leaned back in his chair. "Yes, but that doesn't mean that I don't sympathize."

"I appreciate that. Sympathy is fine. Pity is not."

"No one said anything about pity. Ivy is a sweet girl. I enjoyed getting to know her."

"She is." Her pride in her sister, she didn't try to keep out of her voice.

"Was it difficult growing up? I mean, did kids say ugly things about her around you?"

"Not often. Mostly it was questions. When

we were teens, it was harder. Sadly, I was her only real friend." Lily kept the times she resented Ivy to herself.

"Teenage years can be difficult."

Lily bet Max's weren't. "Even now, I wish she had a wider social circle."

"Ivy is a lot of fun."

With every word, Max made it more difficult to keep her distance from him. Ivy was her soft spot. "Thanks for that. Truthfully I wasn't sure how you would react to her."

"Apparently you've had more than one poor reaction to Ivy. I'm sorry for that. It's not fair to you or her."

"I'm just supersensitive where she is concerned." After all, Ivy needed her to take care of her.

"With your tender heart, that has to be difficult at times." Max took a sip of his water.

Again, he'd impressed her with his observations. "I can be tough when I need to be."

Max grinned. "I don't doubt that. I've been on the receiving end of that toughness."

Why did everything have to circle back to their night—almost—together? Thankfully, the waiter returned with their drinks and to take their meal order.

"What did you want to talk to me about?"

"Why don't we wait until after we eat?" Max suggested.

The waiter arriving with their salads answered the question for her. They ate for a few minutes.

Lily looked around. "I like this place. I'll have to come again. Maybe bring Ivy. She would love the lights. If it were up to her, I'd have to leave the Christmas strands up year-round."

"She'd love my mother's house, then. She has them everywhere. Inside and out."

"That does sound like a place Ivy would appreciate." Lily could imagine the look on Ivy's face.

"What about you?"

"Me?" She met his gaze.

"Yeah. How do you like to decorate for Christmas?"

"I like a real tree with little blue lights, shells and starfish ornaments with little orange beach-chair ornaments here and there."

He chuckled. "That, I hadn't expected. You have a bit of whimsy in you."

Lily halted her fork halfway to her mouth. "Is that your way of saying you think I'm crazy?"

Max's eyes locked with hers. "The last thing I think you are is crazy."

Lily started to ask what he did think of her but was afraid he'd answer too frankly. "Does your family get together every Christmas?"

He lifted a shoulder and let it fall. "Not as often as my mother wishes."

"Most moms feel that way. I know I would."

Max finished the last of his well-prepared steak. He'd enjoyed his meal and Lily's company. They'd settled into small talk about movies they liked, TV shows they watched when they had time, and books they had read. She had an intelligent and quick wit. Something he admired.

Too often the women he went out with were interested only in fashion and how nice his car was. What did his choice in dating partners say about him? Had he become as shallow as they were? He'd spent years trying to grow his career, which left him little time for a real relationship. In truth, he wanted a bond like his parents had but hadn't found the right woman.

His parents were busy people, but they loved each other. As demanding and uncompromising and relentless as his father might be, he'd been a good and devoted husband to his mother. Max couldn't fault his parent in that. It was something Max hoped he'd inherited but feared he couldn't live up to. Maybe that's why he'd always sabotaged his relationships by picking the wrong women—the concern he wouldn't measure up to his father in that area. After all, he was nothing like his father where business was concerned.

Then along had come Lily and her quiet, easy ways, who made him think more about his life. Less about bright lights and more about nights spent at home. Just that quickly he started to dare to peruse the future he hoped for.

People thought him more a playboy than he truly was. He just hadn't found the right person to get serious with. Could Lily be the one? Too many of his friend's marriages had ended in divorce. He didn't want that to happen to his. Especially if it involved Lily. Did he have it in him to make her happy?

He studied her. She was a real woman. Someone who cared deeply for others and was furiously loyal. He wanted a partner to share his life with who fit her profile. Lily was rare. He recognized that. With her, maybe he'd have a real chance.

Max leaned back in his chair, his hands in his lap. "Would you like dessert?"

Lily shook her head. "No, thank you. I've

had plenty and it was wonderful. I'm curious. What did you want to talk to me about?"

He looked around at the tables filled with people. It was best their conversation wasn't heard by anyone. "Why don't we go for a walk? It's a nice night."

"Okay."

As they exited the hotel, Max said, "Let's cross the road and take the beach sidewalk."

"All right. I'm really curious now."

Max grinned. "It's not that big a deal." Or at least he hoped he framed it that way. He had to present the suggestion so Lily didn't think he was doing the same thing Jeff had been trying to achieve. "I guess more of my father has rubbed off on me than I wish to admit. I just don't think our conversation needs to be overheard."

Her eyes narrowed and she leaned in close. "Are we going to discuss the answer to world peace?"

Laughter rolled out of him. He chuckled loudly. When was the last time he'd laughed like that?

Lily's eyes twinkled.

"No, it's not that large." He grabbed her hand and tugged when there was a break in the four-way street. At the walkway on the beach side of the street, he let go of her hand.

"Okay." Lily looked behind and in front them as if they were spies. "I think it's safe to talk now."

He glared at her. "You're making fun of me."

She grinned. "I might be. What's going on?"

He strolled down the walk and she joined him. "It occurred to me that it might be beneficial for us to consider packaging Vseal and Skintec together."

Lily watched him. He looked at her. A suspicious tone filled her voice. "Why's that?"

"Because our products work well together. More often than not, they're needed at the same time. And I believe we can get a better deal if we do."

"I still haven't made any decision." Lily's voice had turned thoughtful.

He stopped. "Good. Please don't until you've talked to me first."

She continued to walk. "Business isn't really my thing. Can I think about it?"

"Sure you can. But just don't take too long. I think it would be to our advantage to announce our decision at the award banquet." Max came up beside her.

"You do?"

"Yeah." At least Lily was hearing him out.

"Do you have someone in mind to package it?"

She asked all the right questions, yet he didn't want her to take his answer wrong. "My father's company has a lot of experience in this area. We'd have more control going with him, I think."

"Wouldn't that be a conflict of interest for you?" She studied him a moment.

Lily might have more business knowledge than she wanted to admit. "No, because I expect to handle working with my father just as if I were doing business with anyone else. He may be a demanding businessman, but he's fair and honest."

"I just need to think about it." She pushed her blowing hair out of her face.

"I don't blame you." They had reached a bench facing the ocean. "Enough about business. Let's sit for a while and watch the sunset."

"That sounds nice." She took a seat beside him but not too close.

The sky had gradually turned orange as the sun moved toward the horizon. They sat in silence a few minutes. He glanced at Lily and saw her shiver. Removing his jacket, he placed it around her shoulders.

She settled into it. "Thanks."

Why did he wish she'd huddle into him like she'd done with the coat?

"Do you watch sunsets often?" Lily said without looking at him.

"No. I can't even tell you the last time I did."

"So why now?"

He laid an arm across the back of the bench but made sure not to touch her. "I don't know. Maybe it's the pace of life here that begs people to slow down enough to do so. Or I just thought it would be something nice to do with you. Does it matter?"

"No. I was just wondering. I've watched you at conferences too. Heard others talk. Just watching a sunset with a woman isn't what you're known for."

"I think you might be surprised to learn that not everything you hear is the truth." His reputation had never bothered him before, but somehow now, it needled him.

"I also have good eyesight."

He chuckled. "I'm not ashamed that I like women."

"From what I've seen, they like you too."

"Is that a note of jealousy I hear?" Max turned so he could better see her.

"Why would I be jealous?" Her tone of innocence didn't ring true.

Max sat a little straighter and gave her a

cheeky grin. "I hope because you find me, uh, interesting."

Lily looked at him for a while before she said, "Maybe a little bit."

His hand slipped down to her neck as his head moved toward hers. He couldn't resist the chance to experience Lily. "Enough that you'll let me kiss you?"

Her lips met his. At first, it was a tentative touch, but she soon showed signs of hunger. He pressed his mouth firmer against hers. She shifted closer as his mouth found the perfect angle to better seal his lips to hers. He restrained his desire, not wanting to scare her with how badly he desired her, had wanted her for too long.

His coat fell from her shoulders as her hands reached to pull him closer. The tip of his tongue brushed the seam of her lips. At her whisper of a sigh, he entered, touching his tongue to hers. She shuddered. Her hands gripped his shoulders. His went to her waist to bring her close. He wanted so much more of sweet Lily.

At the honk of a horn, they broke apart.

Lily quickly shifted away. "Um, I'm…um."

He felt a slow grin came over his face. "That was as nice as I remembered. I've wondered over the last months if I had imagined how great it was."

Lily eyes flickered to meet his. "You have?"

"I have. And I'm not disappointed."

CHAPTER FOUR

LILY DIDN'T KNOW what she had been thinking. She'd returned Max's kiss. She hadn't intended to, but she'd become caught up in the pleasure of kissing him. Her heart still leaped when she thought about his lips meeting hers.

They'd had an agreement. She'd stepped over the line. Those honey-sweet moments of Max kissing her kept running through her mind. There was an attraction between them. One she couldn't let get out of hand by repeating the embrace, even though she wanted to.

There had always been something simmering between them. Even before she really knew him, she'd felt it. He'd drawn her attention, even when she'd stood well across a large room he'd just entered. But she couldn't let that affect her. Becoming enamored of Max James shouldn't be part of her life. It could be her downfall in more ways than one.

Did she dare consider a personal relationship? Their being emotionally involved while joining in a business deal wasn't a good idea. Still, she couldn't help but wonder what it would be like being Max's love interest. In a perfect world it might be possible, but she had Ivy's future to consider. She needed a clear head.

She couldn't spend any more time on worrying about Max. Despite not sleeping much the night before, she managed to get to the hospital early enough to see Mr. Roth before she was due in surgery. Lily headed to his room. She'd almost arrived at the door when she stopped short. Max leaned casually against the wall. "What're you doing here?"

"Good morning to you too."

"I'm sorry. I was just surprised to see you." Her mind had been so focused on Max, she'd not noticed him standing there.

"I came to do rounds. Remember, I'm part of the team for the next few days."

Lily hadn't forgotten. She'd just hoped for a little breathing room, time to think away from him. When he was around, he swallowed up all her thoughts. Now he was doing the same when he wasn't there.

"I wanted to see how Mr. Roth was doing."

"I'm headed to see him right now." She unlocked the office door.

Max followed her in. "I called and checked on him last night. He seemed to be doing a little better."

Wouldn't it be nice if she had someone who cared enough to check in on her? She missed her parents. Her best friend had taken another position out of town six months earlier leaving Lily to her work and Ivy. Maybe it was because she was feeling lonely that Max had such an effect on her. Still, it would be nice to have someone to help shoulder her decisions and worries. What made her think Max would volunteer for that type of position? After all, he was just in town for a few more days.

Lily put her purse away and grabbed her stethoscope off the hook by the door on her way out. "That's good to hear. I only have a few minutes before I'm due in surgery."

"Do you mind if I watch you in action?"

She did, but she wouldn't let him know how much his presence affected her. "I get the feeling you're going to do what you want to anyway."

His mouth went down, creating a comical face. "That hurts my feelings. You know that's not true." His gaze lingered on her. "You'd be surprised by the restraint I have."

His words sent a ripple of awareness along

her spine. Thankfully, the elevator door opening gave her an excuse not to comment.

After seeing Mr. Roth, Lily headed to the surgery locker room. By all indications, her patient was improving. Soon she had her gown on and had entered the OR. She glanced up to see Max sitting in one of the eight seats in the viewing room.

He smiled.

She nodded, squared her shoulders and stepped to the table where her patient waited. Minutes later, she became so involved in the surgery, she forgot about Max and was focused on her job. Confident in her abilities, it still made her nervous to have him watching. For some reason it mattered to her what he thought.

As she prepared to use their products, she thought over what Max had said about joining their marketing strategy. She looked to where he should have been and found him gone. Moving away from the table, she allowed the fellow to close.

While the patient was on the way to recovery, Lily left the operating room, fully expecting to find Max waiting for her in the changing room. He wasn't there. She went to speak to the family, and still no Max.

She returned to her office. Until she was expected in surgery again, she intended to take care of some issues. She had to pay for Ivy's next month at Palm Plantation, the complex where she lived. Lily wanted Ivy to remain there. She had a warm, sheltering place to live, with caring people around her. The problem was that it was expensive. Her parents had left some money, but it would soon run out. Lily had a good job, but not one that would handle paying for her home and Ivy's specialized care. With Max's suggestion they co-market their products, the financial gain might be the answer to her money concerns.

Hours later, she'd finished her straightforward, second surgery, done rounds and was headed home early for the first time in weeks. She'd yet to see Max since that morning. One of her fellows had mentioned he'd seen Dr. James in ICU with Dr. Lee. Other than that, Lily had no word about what Max had done all day. She should've been happy not to have him hanging around all the time. Instead, not knowing where he was made her wonder about him more. It came close to making her angry she not seen him after he been constantly there the last few days.

At home, Lily prepared a salad with the few items she had in her refrigerator and settled in to watch a TV show. Thoughts of Max kept swimming through her head, ruining what should have been her peaceful evening. Lily picked up her phone. He hadn't even bothered to call or text. With a huff, she set the cell on the table. She should be more concerned about keeping her professional distance than with seeing Max again. No doubt he was out doing what playboys did, picking up women. Why did that idea make her sick to her stomach?

How, in such a short time, had Max managed to make her crazy? Instead of thinking about Ivy's needs and what she should do about Skintec, she was spending all of her time on wondering about Max. It had to stop.

Max couldn't help but grin when he saw the surprise on Lily's face when she found him standing beside Mr. Roth's door the next afternoon. Had she missed him? He sure hoped so.

She nodded and entered Mr. Roth's room, then went to his bedside. "How're you doing today?"

"Okay, but I felt better yesterday." The man's coloring wasn't as good as it had been the day before.

"What's different from yesterday to today?" Lily removed her stethoscope from her neck.

Mr. Roth grimaced. "I don't know. I just don't feel right."

Lily put her charting pad down on the end

of the bed. "Let me have a look at you. Your fever seems to be down, and your blood work is looking better. Can you sit up for me?"

Mr. Roth leaned forward.

Lily used her stethoscope to listen to his respirations, then his heartbeat. "All sounds good. I'm going to add another antibiotic. That should take care of your problems."

"I sure hope it does," Mrs. Roth said. "He's starting to be a bad patient."

Lily gave her an encouraging smile. "I'm sure that'll improve when you get out of here. Which I hope is soon."

"Me too," Mr. Roth whined.

"Thanks, Dr. Evans," Mrs. Roth said, patting her husband's shoulder.

Their group moved out into the hall. "Mark," Lily said to one of the fellows, "increase the current antibiotic and add IV erythromycin bid. Let's see if that kills off the problem. That's it for today. See you all tomorrow."

As Lily turned to leave Max fell into step beside her. "How have you been?"

"Fine."

That was a short, curt answer, almost too much so. Was she angry at him? They walked a little farther in silence. "Have I done something wrong?"

Lily faced him. "Nothing, other than you

show up one day wanting my time and attention, then disappear for a day without a word."

He grinned, sidestepping in front of her to see her face clearly. "You missed me, didn't you?"

"I did not." She raised her nose higher. "I just thought it was rude not to let me know you wouldn't be around yesterday." She truly sounded miffed.

"Rude. I'm sorry. I didn't mean to be rude."

"It's just that I wondered at your disappearance. Dr. Lee told me I was to see about you."

They stepped into the elevator. "See about me? I was with her most of yesterday, so she's aware you weren't shirking your duty. This morning I had an appointment."

When the door opened, Lily quickly exited. She threw over her shoulder, "That's good to know. Since you've done so well on your own, then I'll leave you to it. I have work to do."

"One of the fellows was telling me about a restaurant in Little Cuba. I'd like to try it, but it would be so much nicer with company. How about going with me tonight?"

"I don't think I should—"

He wiggled his brows. "Are you afraid you can't resist me?"

Lily's shoulders dropped, and she gave him

a disgusted look. "I've had a long day and have an early one tomorrow."

"You have to eat sometime." He gave her his best pitiful look. "You wouldn't want a visitor to your city to eat alone, would you?"

She took a deep breath and released it slowly. "You're not going to take no for an answer, are you?"

"Not about this. I really hate eating alone." He did. Because of that, he'd had too many of his meals at the hospital. It was one of things he missed about not being in a relationship. Not that he was planning a relationship with Lily. He snorted. Like she'd even give him a chance. Yet that kiss had him daring to hope. "Nope, I don't think that'll happen. When will you be done here?"

"In an hour."

Max grinned. He had her now. "Okay. Why don't I pick you up at your place in two hours?"

"I can drive myself."

He recognized Lily's plan for an early get-away. He wasn't going to let that happen. She needed some fun in her life, and he was going to see to it he provided it. Doing so would let her get to know him better. In turn, she would learn to trust him. That would give him a better chance of convincing her to go along with his plan of packaging their products together.

There might even be a chance of finishing what they'd started at the conference or with that kiss at the beach. Too often, he'd thought about what could have been. He'd like to find out if they would be as good together as he dreamed. "We don't need to take two cars. Just give me your address."

She sighed, then told him what he wanted to know. "Now, let me get my notes added to patient's charts."

"Okay, I'll see you soon." Max left Lily with a bewildered look on her face, while he wore a satisfied grin on his.

For the last two hours, Lily had tried hard to resist the idea that she and Max were going on a date. Yet everything she'd done led only to that conclusion. She'd left the hospital earlier than she'd intended in order to dress for the evening. That had turned into an ordeal. She'd changed four times, finally settling on a simple dress and low-heeled shoes. She'd taken special pains with her hair and applied more makeup than she'd worn in years.

She'd suggested that she drive since she knew the way, and it also gave her some control over the evening. As she pulled up to the front of Max's hotel, she found him waiting.

With a quick look in the rearview mirror, she opened the car door to greet him.

A casual grin rested on Max's lips. "Hello."

"Hey." Lily couldn't help feeling shy. An odd emotion, since she was used to running her world. Around Max, she seemed so unsure. On the occasional, casual dates she'd had since Jeff, she'd known she had no real interest in the men. But for some reason, it mattered too much what Max thought. Why, of all men, did it have to be him?

"You look lovely."

Lovely. Of all the adjectives he could have picked, somehow that one pleased her more than any other would have. Men had told her she was cute, pretty, even beautiful on occasion but never lovely. Coming from Max it seemed more important that the other adjectives. "Thank you. You look like you have gone native."

He glanced down at himself. "I went shopping yesterday. Too much?"

She giggled. Max self-conscious? "I like the beach-shirt-and-shorts look. You fit right in."

"I have to admit I'm a little surprised to see you. I was afraid you'd still be putting up arguments about going with me this evening."

Was she really that easy for him to read?

"I decided if I had to go, then I might as well enjoy it."

"Ouch. Come on." He led her back to the driver's door. "I'm hungry."

"You're always hungry."

He grinned. "I've been saving up for this sandwich all day. I heard it's that good."

She asked, "Do you mind if we put the top down? It's a nice evening."

"Are you kidding? I'd love it. I begged my parents to buy a convertible when growing up. They always said we needed to live in a warm place. As an adult, I understand that. I've resisted buying one too. It isn't practical in Manhattan either."

With the top lowered, they settled in the car.

"What's that look for?" She glanced at him as she put on her safety belt. His brow had wrinkled and his lips had thinned.

"I'm just not used to the woman driving when I take her out." He gave her a chagrined look.

Her heart picked up a beat. "This is a date?"

"When you look like you do, you bet it is."

"Oh, okay." The thrill of having Max say that made her pulse beat faster. "Do you think your self-esteem can stand to have a woman drive you around?"

Max grinned the sexy grin that always pulled at her heart. "I'll try to hold it together."

As she drove Max casually laid his arm along the door and lifted his head into the wind. "This is as good as I imagined."

Lily laughed. "This can't be the first time you've ever ridden in a convertible."

"No, but it's the first time I've been in one with a lovely woman driving."

There was that word again. Lovely. She smiled. "I'm glad you're enjoying it. Tell me where we're going?"

He did, and thirty minutes later, Lily pulled into a parking place near the Máximo Gómez Park. "Give me a sec to put the top up. The restaurant is just across the park and down a block."

As they strolled, Max asked about the people sitting at tables under the trees. "What's going on here? What're they playing?"

"Dominoes."

"Interesting. I've never played the game." Max stopped to watch a moment.

"If you lived around here, you'd have to learn. It's almost the national pastime."

He glanced at her. "Do you know how?"

"Yeah. My grandfather taught me as a child." It had been so much fun playing with him.

"Nice. All these people come here just to

play Dominoes? Is it like this all the time? This must be a tournament."

"Nope. All the time." She led him out of the park across the street. "This is the famous Calle Ocho."

"Eighth Street," Max said, more to himself than to her.

"Correct. This is as Cuban as it gets outside of Cuba. Here's where you can pick up a cigar and a thick cup of black coffee."

Lily inhaled the smell and the sounds. She didn't come here often, but she loved taking it all in when she did. It was like being in another country. As the sidewalk became more crowded, Max's hand came to rest at her waist. When they reached the restaurant entrance, he removed his hand. She missed it immediately. The sense of belonging and security evaporated.

After they were settled at their table and had placed their orders, Max asked, "Have you been here before?"

Lily looked around the courtyard with the bright, festive pennants and small different-colored lights that hung from the palm trees to the building and around the privacy fence. Tall outdoor heaters were stationed in various spots around the space. "No. I've never been here, but I've heard it's very good. I don't get down to this area very often."

"I'm glad I could be the first. I thought some guy might have already escorted you here."

She brushed her hand across the red tablecloth with its blue and yellow stripes. "I don't have much time for a personal life."

Max looked at her long enough that she squirmed in the chair. "Why?"

"Because I have my work. My sister."

He continued to watch her. "Okay, but don't you need more than that? When do you have fun?"

She leaned forward until her chest pressed against the table. "You know, I could ask you the same thing. Or have you got someone who's special who doesn't know you're out with me?"

He followed her move, bringing them almost nose to nose. "I don't cheat. There's no one in my life."

Lily grinned, feeling unusually pleased. "Why not?"

Max leaned back. "Because the right one hasn't come along."

"So you're out for a good time until then?" She had no interest in being another in his long list of women.

He shrugged. "Something like that."

They were interrupted by the server placing their thick Cuban sandwiches in front of them.

"This looks great." Max looked as if he were a dog who hadn't eaten in a week, ready to pounce on the food.

"It's enormous." Lily studied the Cuban bun with so much sliced meat, pulled pork and Swiss cheese piled on that she wouldn't be able to get her mouth around it. "How am I supposed to eat all this?"

Max chuckled. "You can always get a to-go box."

She laughed. "Yeah, and eat it for the next week."

Lily gave up on her sandwich well before Max. She watched as he finished his off. At twilight, a mariachi band took the small stage in one corner of the patio and began playing a rhythmic tune. It floated in the gentle breeze around them. A few couples moved to the open area to dance.

Max took a sip of his drink, then stood and offered his hand. "Will you dance with me?"

Lily's middle tightened as she glanced at the salsa dancers and shook her head. "I'm a horrible dancer. I can't do that."

"Come on. Live a little." Max's hand didn't move.

She pursed her lips. "I'm not making it up. I've never been a good dancer."

"Come on, Lil. I'll take care of you." His gaze urged her to take a chance.

With a roiling stomach, she gave him her hand.

Max pulled her to him and whirled her out to the floor.

"Wow. You do know how to do this."

He gave her wry smile. "Yep. My mother told me one day a girl would be glad I could dance."

"And my mother told me that if I ever found a man who could dance that I better hang on to him."

"Could it be we were meant for each other?" He pulled her close, then whirled her away.

Should she hope that was true? If she didn't live here and Max didn't live thousands of miles away, would they have a chance? If they weren't considering being business partners, maybe? If she could trust him to be the stable man she needed in her life and not a playboy. If, if, if… *Ifs* were too scary. She needed to keep her mind on her career and Ivy. Max was just moving through her life with no intention of staying.

Max enjoyed himself like he never had before. Dancing with Lily was fun. Her head was thrown back, and a smile filled her face as he twirled her away from him and then close. Holding her against him, he rocked back on a foot and she followed as if they had practiced their moves. They seamlessly shifted into a slow song.

"Who told you that you couldn't dance? They were wrong."

"My ex. I never had any training, but I loved to dance until he told me I wasn't any good at it."

Max murmured a harsh word. "Let me assure you he was wrong. He's wrong about other things, as well."

He let his hand dip lower on her waist and brought their hips together. She didn't resist as they moved around the floor in a rocking step. Other couples had joined them, making them have to stay close. Lily's hand on his arm tightened as he led her to the beat of the music. Lily's face was flushed, and her body pliable. His body reacted to her sensual moves. What he wanted from her couldn't be achieved on a dance floor.

The song ended. Lily's dazed look told him she'd felt their sexual attraction too. Max's first impulse was to kiss her, but the crash of a dropped dish jerked him back to where they were. He turned her toward the table. "I think we should be going."

Lily blinked. "Yes, I think that would be a good idea."

Max guided her back to their table. While they waited for the bill, he said nothing and neither did Lily. Not soon enough for him, they were out of the restaurant, away from where the sound of the music urged him to take her into his arms again.

"Let's walk for a while." This was the second time he'd suggested a walk, and he didn't take walks. Somehow, Lily had him wanting to do things he rarely did.

"Okay."

Max took her hand and started down the street in the opposite direction from where her car was parked. The area had become more crowded while they were having dinner. That gave him a good excuse to continue to touch her.

Ahead of them stood a large cream-colored building with a tower on the top. The neon sign beneath read Tower in huge letters. "This looks like an old 1930s theater."

"You are close. It was built in 1925 or 1926. They have redone it. I've not been inside, but I've heard it's nice. Very retro. They show old movies and have film festivals here."

"According to the marquee, The Maltese Falcon is being shown tonight. It's one of my

favorites, but I haven't seen it in a long time."
He glanced at his watch. "What to go?"

"Go?"

"Yeah."

"I really should get home." Lily gave the
building an unsure look.

"Come on. It's still early." Why couldn't she
let go some? Do something spontaneous.

"I guess I could. I usually see movies with
Ivy. It would be nice to see something a bit
different."

He gave her hand a tug. "Then, let's go."

A few minutes later they were seated in the
center of the theater, waiting on the movie to
begin.

"This is one of the best noir films." Max
continued to study the brochure he'd picked
up on their way in.

"Noir?"

He dipped her voice low. "You know the
dark, brooding man and the sultry woman he
loves, but she is bad flick. A crime or mys-
tery film."

"Sounds exciting," she said drily.

"Have you ever seen the Maltese Falcon?"
He stuck the brochure in his pocket.

"Parts of it."

Max turned so he could see her more clearly.

"What? I can't believe it. You've missed part of your education."

She grinned. "And you're planning to correct that."

"I am." The houselights lowered. "Right now."

As the first scene developed, he took Lily's hand and rested his on his thigh. Pleasure filled him when she didn't pull away. Two-thirds of the way through the movie, he felt the weight of Lily's head on his shoulder. She'd fallen asleep.

Something about Lily feeling comfortable enough to nod off on him seemed right. Too much so.

As the credits rolled, he gently shook Lily awake. "Hey, it's time we get going."

"Oh. I didn't mean to nap on you literally and figuratively."

"Not a problem." He chuckled. "I could tell you were glued to the movie."

Lily winced. "I'm sorry. What I saw was good, but I just got so sleepy…"

"I'll try not to take it personally. Let's get you home." He directed her toward the exit.

Half an hour later, they were back in Lily's car, headed toward her house.

Max didn't want to apply pressure, but he needed to know if Lily had given any thought to his suggestion they merge their products. His father had always been good at pushing for what he wanted. Max normally didn't like to, but his father was expecting an answer. "Have you thought about my proposal?"

She stopped for a red light. "Proposal?"

"About packaging our products together."

Lily studied him for a moment with a piercing look. "Is that why you've been cozying up to me? To get me to agree?"

"Cozying?" He raised his brows.

"Yeah. Inviting me to the beach, out to dinner. Being sweet to me. Especially after the fool I made of myself at the conference."

"There was nothing sweet about that kiss we shared. Hot, steamy, unforgettable, maybe, but nothing I'd call cozy." Her soft intake of breath brought him a sense of satisfaction.

"That may be so, but the question still remains. Was tonight about getting me to go in with you to make more money?"

Disappointment filled him. He didn't want to be thought of in the same vein as her ex. "You don't have a very high opinion of me."

"You're still dodging—"

Her phone rang. She pushed a button to use hands-free mode in her car.

"Hello. It's Dr. Evans."

A male voice came through the speaker. "All

of Mr. Roth's vitals are out of line. His white count is up, and he's in pain. Has developed a fever."

"Prep him for surgery. I'll be there as soon as I can."

CHAPTER FIVE

LILY HURRIED DOWN the hospital hall toward surgery. Max kept pace beside her. When she'd offered to let him take her car to his hotel, he'd said, "No, I'm coming with you."

A nurse was busy checking the IV pump attached to the line leading into Mr. Roth's arm when Lily and Max entered the patient-holding area of surgery.

Lily stepped to his stretcher. "Mr. Roth, I'm sorry you're having to go through this. I promise we're going to make you feel better. Hang in there with me. May I have a quick listen to you and have a look at your incision site?"

"Dr. Evans, what's going on?" the man moaned.

"I don't know yet, but we'll soon find out." Lily pulled the stethoscope out of her pocket. Moments later, she listened to his heart rate. "Now, may I see your incision?"

Max stepped up beside her. The area had

turned red and was distended. Lily palpated the area.

Mr. Roth grunted.

"May I?" Max asked. "I'll do my best not to hurt you, Mr. Roth."

The way he moved his hands around the man's midsection showed Max's experience. As he touched the same spot as she had, Mr. Roth reacted.

Lily put a hand on the man's shoulder, giving it a gentle squeeze. "When I see you again, the plan is to have you feeling better." She spoke to the nurse. "I want the latest CBC, electrolytes and liver panel report. I'll be ready to start as soon as I change. Have you seen Dr. Marsh? He's my second tonight."

"He's caught in traffic. Won't be here for another half an hour."

"I'll scrub in," Max said. "I can assist. The board granted me privileges, after all. I might as well take advantage of them."

Relief washed through her. "I'd appreciate it. I don't want to wait any longer. Mr. Roth doesn't have that kind of time."

Max followed her out of the room. As quickly as possible, she and Max were gowned and scrubbed, then standing beside the patient.

"Scalpel, please." Lily said.

The nurse beside Lily confidently handed it to her.

Max stood on the other side of the patient. "My guess, there's a bleeder somewhere."

"But where and why now?" Lily kept her eyes on what she was doing. She efficiently re-opened the area, making an incision just to the side of the original in order to not have to deal with scar tissue. She needed to get in quickly.

"We should know soon enough." A few minutes later, Max positioned the retractor holding Mr. Roth's incision open for their viewing. "Now the hunt begins."

"Yeah." Lily gently shifted a lobe of the liver, looking for the problem.

Minutes crawled by as their heads bent over the open abdomen of Mr. Roth. Lily continued to search as she moved her probe in different directions.

"Wait a sec." Excited notes surrounded the words as Max leaned closer.

"What?" Lily searched but saw nothing.

Max's voice stopped her moment. "I thought I saw something. Lift that spot again. Just as you did before."

Lily did as he said.

"There," he barked. "Got it."

Lily frantically looked. "Where? I don't see anything."

"I only saw the perforation for a second as you moved the vessel." He tilted his head as if trying to find the right angle.

"Mirror," Lily snapped, and the scrub nurse placed it in her hand. She held the glass so that she could see the area Max indicated. "I'm still not seeing anything."

"Let me have the probe." Max put out a gloved hand.

She released the instrument.

"Now, watch." Max shifted the organ to the right.

Joy and relief filled her. "I see it. Just large enough to cause a problem. Let's clean the area and patch it up."

Max's blue gaze met hers over the top of his mask. "I take it you're going to use your patch and my glue."

Her jaw tightened. Was he making a point that once again their products should be packaged together? "I am. Skintec, please."

The nurse presented it in a sterile pan.

"Max, will you hold the edge of the liver just as you have it so I can get this into place." Slowly and carefully, Lily positioned the patch where she wanted it. "Max, hold the flap right there. Glue."

The nurse handed it to her.

Lily sealed the patch. Studying the area carefully, she watched for any indication the repair wasn't secure. She straightened and rolled her shoulders. To Max, she said, "You can relax now."

He stood, as well. "Looks good."

"Yeah. Now let's see if we can find anymore issues." She returned to probing the area. A few minutes went by, then Lily declared, "I'm ready to close now."

An hour later, as she removed her gloves and threw them in the trash outside the OR, Lily said to Max, "Thanks for your help. That was a good spot. I was glad to have you in there."

"You're welcome. I'm sure you would've found it on your own."

"Maybe so, but I still appreciate your assistance." She had. He had been an extra set of excellent eyes.

They finished stripping out of their OR clothing down to their scrubs.

Max threw his soiled garments into the cloth disposal bag. "Not to start a fight, but our products came through again."

"I know, but that never was the issue."

Max pushed the swinging door to step out of surgery. "It's too late and we're both too tired to get into it now. It'll save."

Lily followed and covered a yawn. "I agree. I'm glad I got that nap during the movie."

Max chuckled. "If I'd realized I was going to be in surgery most of the night, I would've joined you in getting some sleep."

"It has been a long day. Give me a few minutes to speak to Mrs. Roth, and I'll drive you to the hotel."

Max looked at the lightening sky of a new day. Most people had been sound asleep in their bed for hours, but he and Lily were just driving away from the hospital. "You live closer than the hotel. I don't want you driving there and back at this hour by yourself."

"I do it all the time." Lily turned right at a light.

"Not with my knowledge. I couldn't in good conscience let you do all that driving. Let me get a couple of hours sleep at your house, then I'll get a taxi to the hotel. I'll be a gentleman. I'll use the sofa. I won't take no for an answer."

"And I'm too tired to argue with you." She yawned.

Insisting he sleep at Lily's might not have been one of his best ideas, but he'd never forgive himself if something happened to Lily on her return trip from the hotel. He'd always taken for granted the women he dated didn't need his help. Lily, he was sure, didn't need it either, but she brought out the desire to protect in him. Something he'd have sworn, up until she came along, wasn't well-developed. He'd spent most of his life being single-minded and career driven, trying to prove he was the best in his field, just as his father was the best in his. Lily made him think of a softer side to life, a less ambitious one.

He was worn out too. Maybe after a hot shower and finding a comfortable spot with a pillow, he'd forget about Lily being under the same roof. Maybe.

Soon, Lily turned into a short drive beside a yellow bungalow. It looked as if it was straight out of the 1950s, with its small porch on the front, wooden siding and coral-colored tropical shutters that stuck out from the house at an angle. Lush flowers bloomed in the front and near the back door. Luxuriant greenery filled the backyard. The place fit Lily perfectly.

In silence, he followed her through a side door into the kitchen. "Nice home."

She placed her purse on the tile-covered counter. "Thanks. It's close to the hospital and is large enough for Ivy and me." She covered another yawn with the back of her hand. "The bath is down the hall. First door on the right. The door across from there is Ivy's room.

You're welcome to it. The sheets are clean. You can have the bath first. I have to feed the cat and let the hospital know I won't be in until this afternoon."

A tabby cat wandered across the white-and-aqua tile of the floor to circle Lily legs.

"This is Poppy. Ivy's cat."

"Hello, Poppy," Max was unsure how to respond, not being a cat person.

"The towels are under the cabinet, along with a spare toothbrush. Make yourself at home. Good night."

He took the hint and headed toward the bathroom. Fifteen minutes later, he stepped across the hall into the bedroom, wearing only his unbuttoned pants. Flipping on the light, he almost groaned out loud. The room's walls were painted a little-girl pink, and a ruffled spread covered the bed. He shouldn't have been surprised. It had to have been picked out by Ivy. As he pulled back the spread, he remembered he'd left his shoes in the bath. Stepping into the hall, he bumped into Lily.

"Ho." His hands held her arms to steady her. "Sorry. I wanted to get my shoes out of your way."

Despite a night in the OR, she smelled like sweetness and the salt of the outside. His gaze met hers. Held. Even in the soft light coming from his room, he could see the interest and insecurity in her eyes. If he kissed her, would it lead to more? Did she want that? Could he afford to have her think he was taking advantage of her? Tonight wasn't the time. He couldn't scare her off.

Stepping back, he put distance between them and let her go, even though his real desire was to pull her against him. "I'll get them when you're done. See you in the morning."

Lily slipped into the bath, and he watched as she gently closed the door behind her. With a lingering look, he closed the bedroom door behind him. He climbed into bed but didn't sleep. Instead, he listened to the water running, then the quiet as he imagined Lily's wet, naked body as she dried off, then put on her night-clothes. Finally, the sound of the door opening and the patter of soft, bared feet going along the wood floor told him Lily was secure in her room.

With a deep sigh, Max punched the pillow beneath his head. He willed his body to relax and tried not to think about his body straining to go to Lily.

By midmorning, Max was cooking breakfast while the stove and the sun heated the cheerful kitchen. He could get used to living in a place like this. No gray days, cold or snow.

He'd been restless for some time, but somehow, being in Lily's home eased his soul. His days had consisted of long workdays, unfulfilling relationships and rare trips to Chicago to see his family. Something about being a part of Lily's life made him want to have someone to commit to, invest in. To care about and have her care about him. Maybe it was time for him to stop drifting through his existence.

Max sensed rather than heard Lily behind him. He continued the rhythmic clink of the fork against the side of the ceramic roll. "I hope I didn't make so much noise I woke you."

"No, I smelled the coffee."

He glanced over his shoulder to find Lily standing in the entrance from the hall. "I have some water hot. I figured you'd prefer tea, based on the amount in the cabinet."

"Thanks. I'll get some after I've checked on Mr. Roth."

Max turned to the eggs. "I've already called. He's stable and had a good morning. The respiratory therapist has already removed the breathing tube. Vitals and labs look good."

Lily had stepped toward him, based on the closeness of her voice. "You've been busy."

Max stiffened at her tight tone. This time, he turned around to completely face her. Lily's hair was mussed, but he could tell she'd tried to push it into some form. She'd pulled on a short housecoat that showed too much leg for his comfort. Her feet were bare. "I'm sorry if you feel I stepped out of my lane. I was just curious. I won't do it again."

She came toward him. "It's okay this time. I should've been up earlier, and then I would've been the one doing the calling."

Max poured the eggs into the hot pan.

Lily reached for a cup and saucer. "So you cook?"

"I do, in fact. Haven't you figured out I'm a bit of a foodie?"

She pulled a tea tin out of the cabinet. "Mostly, I just thought you were hungry all the time."

He grinned. "That too. It helps if you're a foodie."

"I guess it does." She looked over his arm. "What's for breakfast?"

With complete confidence, he said, "My world-famous omelet."

"World famous. Um, isn't that what they all say?"

Max lifted his jaw. "I don't know what others say, but I know what mine tastes like."

She sniffed loudly. "It smells good, but I really should be getting to the hospital."

"I think you've time to eat. It's almost ready

anyway. And I promise you don't want to miss this." He held up a spatula. "Please sit down and I'll serve you."

Lily studied him a moment, then finished preparing her tea before taking a chair at the table.

Max kept his satisfied smile to himself as he slipped the omelet onto a plate and presented it to her with a flourish.

"This is good." Lily held up a forkful of omelet.

"Don't sounded so surprised. I'll have you know I have a number of talents."

Lily's eyes widened. She knew that well. Max was certainly a good kisser. She'd experienced that firsthand, but she couldn't say that. Why did he get to her so? No matter what her mind said, her heart refused to listen where it involved Max. Lily couldn't control her emotions. She liked Max. Admired him, even. She continued to look for ways where he failed, but he always came out being a stand-up guy. Feelings were just feelings. She'd learn to deal.

For now, she'd try to ignore them. "I know you're a smart man. Your glue alone proves that."

Max nodded. "Thank you. Coming from you that's high praise."

Lily held her tongue about them joining sides in marketing their products. She had a sense that he wanted her to say more, but she couldn't. The idea required more thought. Her decision affected Ivy too much for her to make it lightly. Hooking her wagon to Max had too many ramifications to make a snap decision she could regret. She still wasn't convinced it would be her best financial move. Ivy's long-term care would be expensive, and she needed to know she would be taken care of into her old age.

Poppy wrapped around her legs and then around Max's.

Max sat down his coffee mug. "Tell me about Poppy. You said she belongs to Ivy."

Over the next few minutes, they talked about the cat.

Lily put her fork down on the empty plate. "I'll clean up since you cooked, then I've got to get to the hospital. I have surgery that was pushed back to this afternoon. I hate having to do that to my patients. At least it doesn't happen very often."

"You go get ready. I'll take care of the cleanup. I'm dressed. All I have to do is put on my shoes. There isn't much to do anyway. I'll put it all in the dishwasher and start it."

"Thanks." Lily stood. "And thanks for breakfast. You really could be a chef."

He chuckled. "Now you're laying it on a little thick."

Lily wore a smile as she walked out of the room. Who knew it could be so much fun to share breakfast with Max?

Half an hour later, they left her house.

"Would you like me to drop you off by the hotel before I go to the hospital? I've got just enough time to do so."

"I was hoping you'd let me scrub in with you," Max said from the passenger seat.

Lily glanced over at him, her brows drawn together behind her sunglasses. She couldn't imagine him regularly wanting to take a back seat to her or anyone else in the OR. Surgeons by nature were territorial. Max had played sidekick more than once to her, but how long could it continue? Yet she didn't know how to tell him no. "That's fine, if that's what you want to do."

"Afterwards, I need to speak to Dr. Lee, so I'll get my own way back to the hotel."

"Have you and Dr. Lee known each other long? You seem sort of friendly."

"Friendly?" He grinned. "Actually, we worked together in Chicago a few months before she moved to Atlanta and then took the administrative job here."

"I see."

"See what?"

She felt more than saw him looking at her. "Just that you're colleagues."

"Did you think we were involved personally?"

Lily thought of bending the truth but thought better of it. "I might have wondered…"

"Let me set you straight. I wouldn't be going to dinner and a movie with you if I had something going on with Liz. I'm a one-woman man."

"But what we've been doing is about business and me being asked to show you around."

Even with Max wearing dark glasses, she felt his heated glare. "Let me make myself clear, since you haven't caught on. I'm interested in you. The person."

"After that fiasco at the conference, I wasn't sure."

"I thought I had explained that. That Jeff guy really played a number on your self-esteem, didn't he?"

She hated to admit it, but, yeah, he had. "You came along right behind him."

"Ouch. I'm sorry about that. Haven't I proved

over the last few days that I'm not who you thought I was."

"Well, yeah. But I don't know how to tell for sure. I've messed up so badly before."

"You're right. You can't always know, but then you sure do miss out on a lot in life if you don't take a chance on people. Why don't you give me that chance? You might find out that I'm worth it."

She pulled into her parking spot at the hospital. "You think you're that good?"

He shrugged. "You'll never know until you let yourself go enough to trust me. Can you do that?"

"That's a tough request. But I'll try."

He patted the car door, then opened it. "Good. I promise not to disappoint."

"That confident?"

"Nope." He looked back over his shoulder as he got out. "Just willing to work hard to gain your trust." As they walked into the building, he said, "Tell me what's on for surgery this afternoon."

"I have to remove a tumor on a liver." Lily found it interesting that six days ago, it upset her to have Max in the viewing room and now she willingly let him into surgery. "Just remember who's the boss in my OR."

"Yes, ma'am."

An hour later they were in the operating room studying the patient's open midsection.

"This is large and more invasive than the tests indicated." To the nurse standing across from her and next to Max, Lily said, "Suction."

The nurse cleared the area.

"These two large tentacles will need to be cut simultaneously to control the bleeding." Lily looked at Max. "You good with helping with that?"

"Of course."

"I'm going to sever the smaller ones, then we'll do the larger ones last." Lily started removing the tentacles, cauterizing as she went. She felt Max intently watching her procedure. Finished, she handed the cauterizer to the nurse. Looking up at Max, she said, "You ready?"

"Yes." To the nurse standing beside him, he said in a clipped tone, "Scalpel."

She placed it in his hand.

Lily didn't look up. "We'll need to move quickly."

"Agreed."

"All right. Let's get this ugly thing out of here. On my mark. One, two, three." She cut through the vessel attached to the liver while Max did the same on his. Their nurses suctioned the area.

Lily scooped up the thick blob and placed it a pan. "Get it to pathology. Surgical glue."

The nurse handed her the adhesive Max had created.

"Let's get the seams sealed." She worked with speed and caution as she first covered her incision and then the one Max had made. "Now to watch for any bleeding."

An hour and a half later, after closing the patient and seeing her on her way to recovery, Lily and Max removed their surgical gowns.

Lily met Max's look. "I'm glad you were in there with me today. I needed the second pair of hands."

"Happy to be of assistance. I got worried there for a few minutes."

Lily tugged her gown off. "I didn't expect the tumor to be so invasive."

"I gathered that, but you managed the situation well. You did a good job in there."

Lily's phone buzzed. She picked it up off the counter. "Dr. Evans here."

CHAPTER SIX

MAX GRABBED LILY as her face went white and her knees buckled. He pulled her to him, supporting her. "What's wrong?"

She shook her head as she listened to the person on the phone. "I'm on my way… Okay. Okay. Call me with an update every thirty minutes… Have the police been called?"

Fear shot through Max. What was going on?

"Call me immediately if you find her."

His chest tightened. She must be talking about Ivy.

Lily hung up and she faced him, her face drawn with worry. "Ivy's missing. She got mad when she was told she couldn't work outside the compound. She's run away." Lily gulped.

Max tightened his hold.

She sniffled. "Ivy's been gone three hours. They've been trying to phone me all that time, but I was in surgery."

"You should notify the police." He rubbed her back.

"They've already done that."

"Then let's go look for her." Max eased away, ready to head out the door. He couldn't stand the thought of Ivy out there lonely and scared. "We'll find her."

Lily clinched his shirt. "They want me to go home and stay put in case she comes there."

"Then that's what we'll do."

They hurried out of the hospital.

"I'll drive. You're too upset to do so," Max announced as they got into Lily's car. Minutes later they were leaving the parking lot of the hospital.

As they waited at a traffic light, Max glanced at Lily. Her hands remained clutched in her lap, the knuckles blanched of color. A single tear rolled down her cheek. His chest tightened. He laid a hand over hers. "They'll find her, or she'll come home on her own. Hang in there."

Lightning flashed.

"A storm is coming," Lily moaned. "What if she's out in dangerous weather?"

He squeezed her hands. "Don't borrow trouble. She's going to be all right."

"You can't promise that." Lily's voice wavered.

"No, I can't, but they're doing everything

they can to find her, and we're going to do what they asked us to. There's no point in thinking the worst."

Lily's voice wobbled as she said, "All my life I've been told to protect Ivy, watch over her."

"Why was that your job?" Who put that sort of thing on a child?

"Because my parents said she doesn't have a good mind, so that's a reason not to waste mine. 'She can't take care of herself, so you need to help her.'"

Now he understood Lily better. "That's why you're so driven in your work."

"Yes. And I like helping people. Making them feel better. I haven't done a good job this time." She wiped her face with her hands. "I didn't go by to talk to Mr. Roth."

"He'll understand. I'll take care of seeing that one of the fellows checks on him and reports in when we get to your place. Ivy is the most important person right now. You worry about her, and I'll take care of the other stuff."

Max didn't make a habit of taking over a situation and telling anyone what to do, outside his OR or in regard to his patients, but this time, Lily needed his help. He certainly didn't get high-handed with women he was interested in. But it was obvious Lily was on the edge of hysteria by the time they arrived at her house.

He hadn't even turned off the car before Lily was out of it and running through the door, calling Ivy's name. He wasn't far behind. Lily hurried frantically from room to room. Her shoulders slumped with disappointment as she looked at him with watery eyes.

"Where is she?" Lily moaned.

She went down the hall again and back up.

Max's heart went out to Lily. When she reached him again, he took her by the hand and led her into the living room. In front of a cushioned chair, he gave her a nudge to sit. "You need to take a moment. You're going to make yourself sick."

At a rumble of thunder, she shook and looked out the window. "What if she's outside? I need to check the front porch and the yard."

He placed a hand on her shoulder when she moved to get up. "I'll do that. Where's your phone?"

Lily looked at him for a moment like she had no idea what he was talking about. "The kitchen counter. On the kitchen counter."

"Stay right here and I'll get it." He hurried out of the room and returned then handed her the cell. "You stay by the phone while I go out and look for Ivy." He squeezed her shoulder. "It's going to be fine. I promise."

Max stepped out the back door and searched

the yard, looking behind the scrubs. He looked up and down the street of the neat neighborhood. He searched the front porch for any sign Ivy had been there and even double-checked the car in case she climbed in after they had arrived. No Ivy. Where was that girl?

Returning inside, he heard Lily talking. Had Ivy been found? Max stopped in the doorway, hoping he'd overhear good news. She clicked off. By the misery on her face and the way she clutched her phone, it hadn't been good news. "They still haven't found her."

At a crash of thunder Lily jerked, then shivered.

"Come here." Max took her hand, pulling her out of the chair. Wrapping his arms around her, he brought her close and rubbed her back. "Hang in there. You're not alone."

Lily buried her face in his shoulder and hugged him tight. They stood like that for a long time. The room dimmed as the storm approached. Max continued to hold her and whisper soft assurances in her ear.

A long time later, Lily stepped back. "Thank you. Thank you for being here with me."

"Wouldn't be anywhere else." Oddly, he meant it.

Lily returned to the chair.

He watched her wanting to help but not

knowing what he could do. He settled for the practical. "I'm going to get you something to drink. Then I'll fix some sandwiches. All we can do is wait. We'll be here when Ivy comes home."

Rain tapped on the tin roof of the house.

Lily looked out the window. "She shouldn't be out in the rain."

"Ivy's smart enough to find shelter. Don't start imagining more than you know." Max went to the kitchen and prepared Lily a glass of iced tea. He returned to find Lily slumped in the chair, her head lying back as she stared at the ceiling. After setting the glass on the table, he brushed a finger along her cheek.

"My father would be so disappointed in me for not taking care of her."

Max had no doubt she spoke more to herself than him.

"I'm supposed to take care of her. I'm the one with the good mind. It's my job to keep her safe."

Max started to argue, but would Lily listen to common sense in the state she was in? Instead, he returned to the kitchen. Pulling items out of the refrigerator, he prepared them ham-and-cheese sandwiches. He looked through the cabinets and found a bag of chips. After placing a handful on each plate, he carried them into the living room. He sat one plate near Lily, who appeared not to have moved. The other, he put on the coffee table.

She didn't open her eyes. "I'm not hungry."

"No, I guess you aren't. But I don't know how to help other than to care for your practical needs. For my sake, eat two bites." He'd never stayed around long enough with other women to become involved in their emotional issues. Had he been afraid he would fail them just as he'd failed his father? Lily had pulled him into an area where he wasn't comfortable, yet he couldn't leave her.

Lily gave him a weak smile. "That was some speech."

Max shrugged. "But true."

Lily looked out the window at the darkening sky.

He returned to the kitchen for his drink. When he stepped back into the living room, he found Lily eating her sandwich. He took a seat on the sofa. They silently shared their meal. Lily dutifully took her two bites and munched on a chip before pushing the plate away. At a loss for what more to do, Max said nothing. When he finished, he gathered their dishes and set them in the kitchen sink.

Lily said something, but he didn't hear her

clearly. Stepping to the door he asked, "What, sweetheart?"

"It's raining harder. She'll be wet and cold."

Max pursed his lips. He had the best education money could buy. Saved people's lives weekly. Even knew how to enjoy life, but he had no experience that would help him here. He didn't want to disappoint Lily by not being able to help her. "You don't know that." He took her hand. "Come over here and sit beside me."

She joined him on the sofa. He put his arm around her shoulders and brought her next to him. They sat like that for half an hour as the storm blew around them. At the ringing of her phone, they both jumped.

Lily snatched the device up. "Hello... Yes. Yes. Thank goodness... How is she?"

Max squeezed her shoulders, letting Lily know he was there.

She sighed. "Thank heavens. I'll be there in thirty minutes... What? But I need to see her."

Max watched the emotions wash across Lily's face.

"All right. If you think that's the best way. Tell Ivy I'll be there in the morning to take her for breakfast." Lily sounded excited and exhausted as she hung up.

Max turned to face her. "What did they say?"

"She's fine. Wet and cold but fine. She was just outside in the gardener's shed the entire time. She went to sleep."

"Really?"

Lily sighed and slumped back against the cushions, the phone dangling in her hand. "They have her back inside and warm and in her room again."

"Why didn't they want you to come see her?" The relief he felt could only equal Lily's. The Evans women had begun to matter to him a great deal.

"They don't want me upsetting her. She's calm and safe, and they want it to stay that way."

"I can understand that." He wanted Lily to feel the same.

"They have her settled. She was scared, as well. They're afraid it'll be too much if I show up. She might get upset again. Ivy knows they called me."

Max took her hand. "That makes sense."

"They suggested I come have breakfast with her in the morning. That's not all that unusual. I do it when I'm going in late."

Max hugged her and kissed her temple. "I'm glad she's home and safe."

"Me too."

He searched her face. "How're you doing?"

"I'm okay. Now." Her eyes still swam with tears. "It'll take a while for the adrenaline to settle. I'll drive you home in a few minutes."

"No hurry. I'll stay as long as you need me." He pulled her back into his arms. "We'll sit here for as much time as you want." The storm had settled into a steady beat on the roof. "This is nice anyway."

Lily turned so that she met his gaze. "Thank you for staying with me. I don't know what I would've done."

"You're one of the strongest women I know. You would've handled it. But I'm glad I was here." Max found he meant it. He wanted to be there for her.

"I'm not strong where my sister is concerned."

"I don't think any of us are strong where our family is concerned." He certainly had a hard time standing up to his father. Even now, Max still felt he had to prove himself.

She laid her head on his chest and sighed. "You're a nice guy, Max James."

"Was there ever any doubt?"

"I had some for a while, but you've proven you're different than I first thought." She looked at him a moment before settling against him again.

"I'm glad you think so, but don't put me up on a pedestal because I get air sickness and it'll be easy to fall off."

"Sometimes you can't help how you feel," she said softly.

Max could certainly identify with that. He felt too much for Lily. Far more than he'd ever dreamed he could. What started out as a family situation was quickly developing into a personal one. A relationship that involved more than a one-night stand or getting her to go along with them packaging their products together.

Lily snuggled into him.

His breath caught when her lips touched his neck. He couldn't think of another time she'd voluntarily touched him since he'd known her. "Lily?"

"Yes?" Her lips continued along his skin.

"Don't play with me."

"What do you mean?" she murmured against his ear.

"You know exactly what I mean."

She kissed his neck again. "You mean this?"

"Yeah." He groaned. Did she realize what she was doing to him?

"I was just saying thank you." A teasing note circled the words. She kissed his jaw.

"You've just had a scare. You're not think-ing like yourself."

Her hand came to rest on his chest. "I was thinking of celebrating."

"How were you planning on doing that?" He wasn't used to this aggressive Lily, but he found he really liked the idea of it.

"Before I tell you, I need to know if you'd be willing to celebrate with me." Her hand moved over his chest.

"I'd need to know what's involved before I answered that question."

"Such a careful man. I was thinking if it was all right with you, I'd like to kiss you."

Max sucked in a breath. "I think you need to be careful about what you're doing. There's a real chance I won't stop at a kiss."

Lily turned so their gazes met. "I'll take that risk."

Max looked around at the dimly lit room, giving his heart a moment to steady its beat and his mind time to think straight, because he had every intention of kissing her senseless.

Lily held her breath as she watched Max. Had she just embarrassed herself with him again? Was this his way of telling her he wasn't in-terested?

She'd made only a slight move when his arms tightened, and his mouth found hers.

Max's body remained tense, as if he were holding himself back, as if judging if he should take the kiss deeper. She suspected she'd made him question himself because of her attitude about what had happened between them before.

She wanted all his passion. Didn't want him to hold anything in reserve. Tonight, she needed to break out and feel alive. To forget her responsibilities. To be swept away by his touches and kisses.

Sliding her hand across the plane of his chest to the nape of his neck, she ran her fingers though his hair and nudged his head closer in encouragement as her mouth opened. Max took her invitation. His tongue brushed hers, causing a tingle to ripple down her spine. She shivered. Could anything feel better than Max's kisses?

His hand slid up her back and down again as his mouth left hers and skimmed over her cheek. To travel to her temple. "Lily, you taste as magical as I dreamed you would."

She leaned her head to the side, giving him better access to her neck. Her heartbeat tapped faster as he kissed behind her ear. She moaned, leaning closer to Max.

His arm scooped up her knees and he lifted her across his lap.

Lily pressed her chest against his as her hands cupped his face. Her mouth found his again. Being so forward wasn't like her, but Max's eager return of her attention made her bold. Kissing Max was all she dreamed it might be and more. She wiggled against him and wasn't disappointed to find the thickness of his desire pressing against her hip.

His arms tightened at her waist as he took over the kiss. With tongues in a tangle, he lay her on the sofa and bent over her. Her hands kneaded the muscles of his back as she returned his kisses. Her blood hummed through her veins. She'd never felt this heated need before. It made her confident. Had her wanting… more. Max. It all.

A large warm hand cupped her hip, bringing it more securely beneath him. His hand slipped under her shirt until his palm lay on her stomach. Her muscles tightened as his fingers worked their way upward. His mouth released her long enough to nip at her bottom lip.

"Mmm, I can't seem to get enough of you."

Lily squirmed. She kissed his chin, then his jaw, rough with its afternoon growth. It only added to his appeal and her appreciation of their differences.

Max placed light kisses on her eyes, fore-head and found that sweet spot behind her ear that made her moan with delight. As his mouth worked its charms, his hand continued its exploration of her middle on the way to her breasts. One of his fingers followed the line of her bra from left to right before returning to the deep V where the front clasp was located. With a practiced flip of thumb and forefinger, he released her bra.

His mouth left hers and he looked at her with a flame of desire flickering in his eyes. "Okay?"

She wasn't sure whether he was asking about her feelings or if it was okay to open her bra, but the answer was the same for both. "Better than okay."

The hand that had stilled on her ribcage nudged her bra away. He cupped her breast. In a hushed tone he whispered, "So sweet. So perfect."

Air escaped her lungs in a whoosh. Her nipples tightened, and her breast tingled in antici-pation of his attention.

"This shirt belongs somewhere else."

She raised her arms. Max pealed the mate-rial over her head and dropped it unceremoni-ously to the floor. He brushed her bra straps away and looked at her.

Lily watched his eyes. They never left her. She couldn't remember being more exposed or desired in her life.

Max's gaze rose. Seconds later, his lips met hers in a gentle, controlled kiss that made her stomach flutter and her core heat. One of his hands supported her head, his fingers buried in her hair. His other hand eased over her mid-section as if he were memorizing the dips and curves of her body. She quivered as he left a path of heat in his wake. Her breath came in puffs as she waited, anticipating him touching her aching breasts.

His mouth left hers. He kissed her cheek, the ridge of her shoulder, the top of a breast before his mouth found her nipple.

The breath Lily hadn't realized she was hold-ing, rushed from her lungs. As Max's tongue tugged and teased, her center tightened and throbbed. Oh, what Max's touch did to her. The contact was electric. She whimpered.

His roguish look met hers. "You liked that?"

She nodded, unable to form a word.

He cupped and lifted her other breast. "Let's see if you like this better." His thumb grazed her nipple before his forefinger circled it.

Lily hissed from the heat swirling through-out her body caused by his attention. Why did Max, of all men, have such an effect on her? Her hands tightened on his shoulders, kneading his muscles as his lips followed the path of his fingers. His mouth continued its magic while her fingers moved to his waist and worked their way under his shirt.

At her admistrations, his body tensed. His skin rippled as her fingertips drifted over his ribs and along his back. Lily kissed the top his ear. "I think this shirt should go."

He leaned back on his knees, jerking his shirt over his head. It quickly landed on the floor.

Lily wasted no time in running her hands across his chest, teasing the light dusting of hair there, before he lowered himself against her again. As her skin met his, Max's lips found hers. She joined his heated kisses with those of her own.

She wanted all Max could offer.

Max's mouth slanted across Lily's. He couldn't get enough of her. Her sweet kisses. Her sexy body. Her sinuous touch. Everything about her called to him. He'd known that night at the conference there was something different about Lily, something special. A piece he was missing in his life. He wanted to discover it, experience it.

As his tongue tasted hers, Lily lifted her

hips to meet his thick and straining manhood beneath his pants zipper.

Headlights of a car from the next-door neighbor's drive arced around the room.

Max lifted his head. Lily's living room, with the large, low windows, wasn't where they should be when they took this to the next stage. He didn't mind being a bit of an exhibitionist, but he had no doubt Lily wasn't into it.

"I think we need to take this to a place a little more private." Max sat back and pulled her up beside him. He handed Lily the first piece of clothing he came to, which was his shirt.

Lily slipped it over her head. Standing, he looked down at her. Would she put an end to the direction they were headed because of the interruption? He wouldn't pressure her to go where she didn't want to go, even if it might kill him.

Her gaze met his and she placed her hand in his. "Would my bedroom work?"

"It would be a good start."

She giggled. "Did you have somewhere else in mind?"

He grinned and raised a brow. "The kitchen table?"

She tugged him toward the hallway. "I'm thinking someplace softer."

Max bumped into her when she stopped abruptly as they reached her doorway.

"Are you okay?" He looked over her shoulder and searched the room.

"I just wanted you to know I don't bring men here."

Max placed a hand around her waist. Pulling her back against him, he nuzzled her neck. He needed to get them back to where they'd been. "I'm honored to be invited. Would you show me around?"

"Huh?" Lily stepped farther into the room. "There isn't much to show."

What he was particularly interested in was the bed. "No hot pink and ruffles. I'm a little disappointed."

Lily gave him a silly grin. "Ivy and I don't share the same décor taste."

"And I'm glad." He glanced around.

A bed with an upholstered yellow headboard faced the door. A spread in light blue and yellow covered it. An antique-looking nightstand with a lamp was positioned to the right. That must be Lily's side of the bed. In front of a double window sat a desk with a floral-cushion chair in the same colors as the spread. An old-fashioned wardrobe that had been painted a cream color was positioned on another wall.

She went to the windows and closed the colonial blinds, shutting out the world. The only light in the room came from the hall.

He sat on the bed. "Lily, will you come here?"

She studied him a moment. That aggressive woman in the living room had turned shy.

Max waited, patient outside but eager inside. Finally, she stepped toward him. She stopped an arm's length away. He took her hand and led her to stand between his legs. "You're cute in my shirt."

Lily glanced down. "I should've put mine on."

"Why, when I'm just going to take it off?" His hands went to her waist and slid up under the garment, gathering it as he went. "You're too amazing not to admire."

Lily lifted her arms, and he removed the shirt. His hands went to her hips and nudged her forward. He needed to touch her. Seconds later, his mouth found a nipple. Her fingers came to his shoulders, the nails biting into him. She moaned and leaned her head back. His manhood went rock-hard.

Max moved his mouth to her other breast. Finding the button of her pants, he released it, then pushed the material down her legs. He continued exploring her body as he removed her panties, then guided her onto the mattress beside him. The dim light washed over her beautiful curves. Lily took his breath away.

"You are so lovely." His mouth found hers.

Wrapping her arms around his waist, she tugged him to her. She shifted beneath him, her center finding his hard length, and pressed against him.

"Lily, I don't want to rush this, but if you keep that up, I'll be done before we start."

She smiled softly.

He placed a hand on her stomach. "I want to touch more of you."

Her gaze locked on him as his hand slid lower. Her muscles tensed beneath his palm as it wandered over her. Her fingers traveled across his chest. He teased her curls, and she lifted her hips. Max moved his index finger between her legs. For a moment, her legs tightened, halting the advancement. His mouth returned to hers and she relaxed. Unable to stand it any longer, his finger found her opening and entered.

Lily quivered, which only increased his need. Yet only her pleasure was his concern at that moment. Max pulled away. Lily made a sound of complaint. He reentered her and she flexed to meet him. His mouth found a breast once more. As he suckled her nipple, he continued the push-and-pull motion between her legs, enjoying Lily's grip on his finger.

She squirmed, her hips lifting. Seconds later, her back stiffened and she whimpered her release.

Max gazed at Lily. His heart thumped against his rib cage. Pride filled him. He'd put that look of pure bliss on her face. Had he ever seen anything so beautiful? He could watch that every day for the rest of his life.

"Aren't you going to take your pants off?" Lily's hand moved to the button of his shorts, which were barely containing his throbbing flesh.

When her small hand grazed the bulge as she worked to release the button, he came close to losing his tentative control.

"I think I better do that." He stood. Pulling his wallet out, he removed a condom, then stuffed the wallet back into his pocket. He quickly flipped the button open, unzipped and pushed his pants and underwear to his ankles before stepping out of them. As he moved, Lily watched him with her eyes wide and her bottom lip between her teeth.

He rolled on the protection. "Honey, I don't think I can wait any longer. I want you too badly."

She leaned up, took his hand and gave it a tug. "I want you too."

Max came over her where she lay in the middle of the bed. His mouth found hers as his manhood touched her entrance. With a flex of his hips, he entered her wet, heated center. He pushed deeper. Lily lifted to meet him. He pulled back and slid in fully. Her legs circled his waist, fixing him more securely to her.

His world swirled around him as he forgot everything but Lily and the pleasure building like hot lava within him. Her fingernails scraped across his back as she wiggled closer, then tensed before keening her delight.

Max grasped for his release, plunging deep and steady. With a grunt of supreme satisfaction, he found an orgasm like he'd never experienced before.

The rain continued to fall outside, and night had settled in. Lily snuggled into the warmth of Max's side. Her head lay on his arm. At her movement, his hand came to rest on her shoulder.

He vaguely remembered pulling the covers back and helping her under them before he joined her, pulling her close. Did he dare wish for this contentment to continue? No, he couldn't think like that. He would be gone in four days.

"What're you thinking?" Max's husky voice rumbled.

"How do you know I'm thinking anything?"

"Because I can feel the change in your body." His words were matter-of-fact, as if his explanation was a given.

Was he that in tune with her? He never experienced that before.

"I was just wondering…"

An emotion resembling fear filled him. Max rolled so he faced her. Even in the dim light, she could see his eyes watching her. Concern filled them. "Do you want me to go?"

Her chest tightened. "I thought you might want to."

Max brushed her cheek with the back of his hand. "I don't want to be anywhere but with you. Right here."

"That's nice, but I can't get used to having this. You're leaving in a few days."

"Yeah, but there are airplanes and long weekends, and—" he grinned "—conferences. Right now, why don't we not worry about the future and just enjoy the here and now? I have other things I'd rather be doing." He trailed a finger over her shoulder and down to her breast where he circled her nipple.

He enjoyed Lily's sweet shivered. Was it wrong to wish for more moments like this?

CHAPTER SEVEN

LILY'S EYES POPPED open at the feel of warm flesh beneath her hand. *Max.* He was still there. She wasn't used to waking up next to a man, especially a naked one, but she had to admit she liked it. Too much.

She'd certainly appreciated his support while Ivy was missing. Living through that nightmare without his encouragement would have made the situation unbearable. Jeff would have never been there for her like Max had been. Could she let go and believe he could be with her for more than just sex?

Even her parents had missed the signals where her emotions were concerned. They had loved her, but their focus had been on Ivy so much of the time. Max seemed to see her, understand her.

A large hand brushed across her hip.

She stopped herself from purring like a kitten. She looked over to find Max watching her. "You're still here."

"I said I would be. I thought I had proven you can trust me."

She lifted a shoulder. "But after last time…"

"You can't blame all of what happened on me."

"I guess not." Some of it had been her responsibility. But at the time, she hadn't been able to see that. She's wouldn't think about him maybe not being all she hoped for. She subconsciously harbored insecurity issues where he was concerned. "What time is it?"

She'd always had a good internal clock, but somehow when she was with Max, she lost track of time and everything else. He was changing her. Was that good or bad?

"Somewhere around seven, I think."

She threw off the covers. She'd forgotten she wore nothing and quickly picked up Max's shirt and jerked it in front of her.

"You do know I've seen and touched all of you." His eyes held a wicked gleam.

Heat washed over her body.

"You fascinate me. You're this take-charge woman everywhere but where your personal life is concerned. I'm sorry I had a part in making you so insecure. That was never my intention. From the first time I saw you, I thought you were someone special."

Her heart opened and took him in. Max's words were balm to her aching self-esteem. "That's sweet of you."

He rolled toward her, the sheet going low on his hips. "I'm not being sweet, I'm telling the truth."

"Thank you." As much as she would've liked to crawl back into bed, she couldn't. "I've got to go. Ivy gets antsy if she has to wait, and I need to see for myself she's okay."

"I don't blame you. I tell you what, while you get ready, I'll call the hospital and check on our patients."

She pulled his shirt over her head. "I plan to go in after I see Ivy."

He pushed the covers away and sat on the edge of the bed. "Take the day off. You've done an all-night surgery and worried over your sister, back-to-back. Even you aren't superhuman."

She forced herself not to push his shoulders back to the bed and climb on him. A naked Max in her bed, saying words she needed to hear, almost made her forget her responsibilities. "I have patients who depend on me."

"Yes, they do, and from everything I can tell, you have good fellows. Let them handle today. There are excellent nurses and all the other staff there to take care of them. You're just a phone call away if you're needed."

She placed her hands on her waist. "Are you telling me what to do?"

"Uh, no." He shook his head. "I'd never make that mistake. I'm merely suggesting. Come on, Lily. Cut yourself a little slack for once. You've already left a message with your nurse to reschedule your patients. Let's do something fun."

She went to her dresser and gathered her underwear. He did tempt her. She had him only a few more days after all.

"I'd like to spend the day with you." His eyes held a wicked gleam.

Lily couldn't disagree, but she should be careful not to get used to such attention. She stepped to Max, placing her hand on his chest. "I would like to, but I don't play hooky from work. People depend on me."

He removed her hand and kissed the palm. "Neither do I, but I do think you need a mental-health day, and you've already taken off this morning."

She screwed up her mouth and shook her head.

"I tell you what. Why don't you take the rest

of the day off, and we'll stop in and see your patients this evening. Would that work?"

"Deal." She put out her hand.

Max stood, in all his naked glory, his hands going to her forearms. He looked into her eyes. "I'd rather seal it with a kiss."

Lily leaned into him as his lips found hers. She clung to his shoulders as he took the kiss deeper.

"How much time do we have before you have to leave?" He asked between nips on her lips.

"Not long enough." She pushed away.

Max wiggled his brows and gave her a sexy grin. "We could save time by sharing a shower?"

At eleven, Max parked in front of Lily's house. She'd dropped him off at his hotel on her way to see Ivy. She'd told him she'd call him when she started back to her house. Her car wasn't in the drive, but he expected her soon.

Their night together had been more than he'd ever thought it might be. Lily had been his dream lover, willing, responsive, caring and just a little timid. He wasn't the type of guy who spent the night with a woman, few in fact, but Lily had him wanting to hold her for hours. All through tonight and tomorrow night, forever.

Forever?

At one time, he'd thought of marrying but as time moved on and no woman fit his ideal of what he wanted or needed, he'd let the idea drift by. He had no interest in the women his father thought would fit the James name. Despite that, he'd continued to date the splashy, socialite type, hoping he'd find someone who would fit his needs and please his father. Then he'd seen Lily at a conference. Her quiet, easy ways interested him, but sensing her wariness, he'd not approached her until that night. He sighed. What would his life be like now if he'd gotten to know her years ago?

But now the idea of marriage had returned as something he could embrace. In reality, he just wanted Lily any way he could have her. The question was: Did she feel the same?

His phone rang. The screen showed his father's name. Max braced himself, then answered. "Hi, Dad."

"Max, I was just checking in to see if you have convinced that woman to package her product with yours. We have to start marketing it soon."

Max's mouth drew into a thin line before he

took a deep breath. "I'm doing fine. Thanks for asking."

"This isn't the time to be joking, Max. This is a big deal and could send our company into Fortune 500 status."

"Dad, it's not my company. It's yours. I'm a doctor."

"You know what I mean. I could use your medical insight on this project if you'd give it, but first we have to get her product."

"That *her* has a name. Dr. Lily Evans." Max didn't like his father treating Lily as if she and her feelings were unimportant. He didn't appreciate having it done to him, and he sure wasn't letting his father do it to Lily.

"Max—" his father's voice held a whiff of irritation "—have you or have you not spoken to her about the partnership?"

"I have."

"What did she say?"

"She's thinking about it." Which Max had encouraged.

"Then, nudge her along. I need this deal."

"I've already agreed to let you have the production of my glue. You don't have to have Lily's patch."

Everything with his father was a transaction. The only deal he'd never been able to make was the one keeping his son from following in his footsteps. Max had been called to medicine, and his father had done all he could to stop Max from following that dream. Max had been groomed as next in line to lead The James Company. His father hadn't given up on pulling him into the business, even after all these years. The problem remained that Max carried guilt over disappointing his father. He'd hoped his discovery of the glue and giving it to his father's corporation for production would improve their relationship. Sadly, he wasn't so sure that could or would ever happen.

His father continued as if Max had said nothing. "Yeah, but with the patch we could triple the price and demand."

Apparently, once again, what Max had accomplished wasn't good enough.

"Dad, I get it, but I know Lily, and pushing her isn't going to make her say yes until she's ready. If she ever agrees."

"You're calling her Lily. That must mean you know her pretty well?"

"We're friends." More than friends. He was thinking about a future with her that had nothing to do with his father's aspirations. Max had no interest in hearing his parent's view of Lily.

"Then use some of that charm I've heard about with women and get me a positive answer."

Anger bubbled in Max. He would never *charm* Lily into doing something she didn't want to do. With her he wasn't that playboy everyone said he was. "Dad, it's been good talking to you. See you soon. Bye."

His father said something, but Max had finished listening.

A tap on the window drew his attention. Lily's face was framed there. Max stepped out of his vehicle.

"I was wondering if you planned to get out of the car. Everything okay?"

"Sure it is." Max pushed his father's words away and smiled. "You're here, aren't you?"

She huffed. "Now you're turning on the Dr. James irresistible charm."

He put his arm around her waist and gave her a quick kiss. "You think I'm irresistible?"

Lily laughed. "You aren't going to trick me into feeding your ego."

They started toward the house.

As she opened the back door, she asked, "Now that we have the afternoon free, what do you want to do?"

He followed her inside. "I hope you don't mind. I already have something planned."

"You have?" She placed her purse on the table.

"Yep."

She faced him. "What're we doing?"

"You'll see. Bring your bathing suit. We should have a chance to swim." As Lily started down the hall, he lightly patted her on the butt. "Hurry."

Half an hour later, Max pulled into a marina. He took Lily's hand as they walked down the long pier. He couldn't have asked for a nicer day. The sky was clear, and there was a light breeze. Something had broken in him, falling away while being with Lily. She brought an easiness to his life. Acceptance was what she gave him. It soothed his soul.

"What're we doing here? Are we getting on a boat?"

Max squeezed her hand. "So many questions? Don't you like surprises?"

"I do, but—"

He gave her a quick kiss. "Then, be surprised."

Six slips down on the right, they stopped beside a yellow cigarette speedboat. Max climbed on.

"We're going somewhere in this?" Lily's voice rose an octave higher as she looked in wonder at the watercraft with the long, sleek, V-shaped hull.

"We are. You coming?" Max lifted his hand.

She grinned and took it. "Sure I am."

Max chuckled. Lily had a bit of an adventuress in her. He liked that. It had shown some in the shower this morning, but it was increasingly coming out now. Was there more where that came from? He hoped to find out.

He helped Lily down. She came to stand between the two captain chairs and the bench seat behind them. Lily placed her hand on the windshield, which ran from side to side across the craft. "Wow. This is some boat."

"I'm glad you like it." Max climbed out and released the bowline, then the stern ropes before climbing back in. Taking the driver's seat, he started the engine, which roared, then settled into a purr. He had to agree the boat was a fine water machine.

Lily settled into the other seat with a look of amazement on her face. "I've never been on a cigarette boat."

"You've lived in Miami for years and never been out on one of these?" He maneuvered out of the slip.

Lily shrugged. "I haven't had a chance or anyone to go with. You do know how to handle a boat this powerful?"

Max stood to see the water around them as they moved at idle speed out of the marina. "I do. I own one similar at home. Happier now?"

"An ocean is a lot different than the Hudson River or the East River in New York." She looked at another boat passing them, going in the opposite direction.

"Big water is still water. We aren't going that far out. Settle back and enjoy the ride. You worry too much."

"Somebody has to think about these things." Lily eased back in the chair, looking more relaxed despite her words. "Since people like you don't seem to let anything bother you."

Little did she know. "Hey, I didn't mean to start an argument. The afternoon is too beautiful to waste bickering. But then again, I might enjoy making up."

Lily felt heat washed over her. She had no doubt from Max's grin that he'd been rewarded by her blush, which had nothing to do with the sun beaming down on them. Sex with Max had been… She had no words. Freeing, liberating, extraordinary, mind-blowing. Maybe she did have words, but they were inadequate. He'd been attentive, caring, tender. Max had seen to her pleasure before he'd considered his own. She'd had no idea what sex could really be like until Max. He'd made sure she felt desired and satisfied again and again.

She would have described herself as a conservative sexual partner until she'd had sex in the shower with Max. In fact, that had been another of Jeff's complaints about her. Max hadn't seemed disappointed. She smiled. From the way Max acted, she had satisfied him, completely.

But more than that he'd been there for her when Ivy had been missing. Jeff had been all about himself. His job, his problems and his pleasure. He would have never spent an evening with her if there had been a problem with Ivy. Max was so much more of a man than Jeff had ever been. She had wasted too much time mourning Jeff's leaving. Instead, she should be glad he wasn't in her life anymore.

Max had opened an entire new world for her. She looked at him. Even now, he had her body at a low hum. It excited her.

Despite her initial guilt of not going to the hospital, she was enjoying herself. The day couldn't be more beautiful, and she'd never felt better about life. She was having fun. When was the last time she'd been able to say that?

"Have you spent any time boating?" Max glanced at her, then looked back at the water ahead.

"What?"

"Boats. Do you know anything about them?" Max had caught her daydreaming. Of him.

"Not much, but I love them. I like being out on the water."

"When we're out into a less-congested area, how would you like to drive?"

A thump of excitement filled her chest. "Could I?"

Max gave the boat a little more speed. "Sure. Do you know why they call this a cigarette boat?"

Lily pulled a hat out of the bag sitting at her feet and put it on her head. "No. But by the look on your face, you do."

"I do. The boat design reminded the inventor of a cigarette. Long and sleek. Hold on to your hat. I'm going to give it a more speed." Max pushed the throttle forward.

They moved out into more open water.

Lily placed a hand on top of her head to prevent the hat from blowing off, then raised her chin, appreciating the wind and warmth of the sun. A thrill went through her as she they skipped over the water, the small waves making a thumping sound against the hull.

Max pulled back on the speed as they approached a wide inlet.

"Is something wrong?" she called to him.

"No."

"Then, what're we doing?"

He grinned. "I thought you might like a water tour of the rich and famous."

She stood up beside him, holding tight to the top of the windshield. "That sounds like fun."

Max slowed the boat to a crawl.

"How did you know where to come?"

He pulled a piece of paper out of his back pocket and grinned. "The marina master gave me some ideas. What did you think? I'd give you a cheap tour?"

"I never doubted you for a moment."

"Now, this house up here on the right belongs to a famous singer. The guy at the marina couldn't remember her name."

Lily laughed. It felt so wonderful to do so. For once, it was good to be alive. Think or not think about something besides work and Ivy.

"This next one belongs to a baseball player." Max pointed to one pale pink mansion whose bright green lawn came to the edge of the water, where an inboard motorboat rocked against a pier.

"It's gorgeous, isn't it?" Lily studied the place that reminded her of a gleaming jewel.

"How about this next one? A football player lives there."

She laughed. "How did you guess that, given the football goal in the yard?"

Max teased. "Hey, you have to give your tour guide some credit."

The wind picked up and Lily said, "Let me have that paper so you can drive."

He handed it to her as they continued to troll along the narrowing waterway.

Lily pointed to a house farther down. "I like this one. The yellow and cream. Let me see who lives there." She searched the list. "I can't find a name for this one."

"Apparently, someone rich but not famous." Max made a wide turn and headed back the way they'd come but staying to the other side of the channel.

"These are really beautiful houses with amazing yards, but they are too much…" She watched the houses going by.

"Too much what?"

"Too big, too much to clean, too many taxes."

Max looked at her. "You wouldn't like to live in one of these?"

Something about the way he asked the question made her think her answer mattered to him. "Heavens no, I really love my bungalow."

"I like it too. It feels much more like home than my apartment." His attention stayed on the water.

"I bet yours is in one of those ultramodern apartment buildings on the top floor."

His mouth quirked upward on one side. "It's on the second floor from the top. I don't spend much time there. Mostly, it's a place to eat, dress and sleep."

"I bet you're out on the town all the time." She didn't like to think of him with other women. It hadn't taken but one night with him to make her possessive.

He chuckled. "More like, at the hospital or in a lab."

"I thought you were a good-time guy." Lily tried to sound teasing, but her tone made her words fall flat.

"You can't believe everything you hear."

Her attention turned away from the houses to him. "Then, tell me something true about yourself."

"I like to think I'm a good guy. Dependable, honest and loyal."

She liked his answers. From what she could tell, they were true. "Those are all great qualities. If you weren't a doctor, what would you be doing?"

"I guess I'd be working in my father's company. That's what he groomed me for."

She noted the undercurrent of negativity in his voice. "But you didn't want that?"

"No, much to his disappointment. I've

wanted to be a doctor since I was a kid and broke my arm when I fell out of a tree."

"You fell out of a tree? How far up were you?" Lily turned to see him clearly.

"In the top. It wasn't a supertall tree, but it was high enough."

She wanted to know about the boy he had been. "How old were you?"

"Eight, almost nine."

She could imagine a young Max with missing teeth, a grin and laughter in his eyes. "What did the doctor who set your arm do that made you decide then to become a doctor?"

"I don't know that it was him per se, but the idea that he could put something broken in the human body together again amazed me. I thought then I'd like to do that. There's a wonder to our work. Even today, I feel it."

Lily like this thoughtful side of Max. The one who was in awe of and had pride in his work.

"But not everyone sees it that way."

"Like whom?" Who wouldn't see how great Max was as a person and a doctor?

"My father."

"He doesn't like you being a surgeon?" She couldn't believe that. Max had too much talent to not be doing surgery.

"He'd rather me use my medical knowledge and clout to help expand his company."

She saw his hands tighten on the steering wheel. "And you have no wish for that?"

"Not even a little bit. I've never had any interest in business. I like the hands-on of operating. Of working with people. I hate paperwork, which I'm reminded of by medical records often. But my father can't seem to accept that, even to this day."

Lily shook her head sadly. His bitterness rang clear in his voice. "It would be a huge loss to the liver-transplant community if we lost you."

Max's bright smile brought one to her lips. "Thanks for that. It's nice to know someone has faith in me." He gave her hand a quick squeeze. "You better sit down. I'm getting ready to speed up."

She took her seat and held on to her hat as they sped across the water. When they were away from the boat traffic and in open water, Max slowed and stopped.

"Is something wrong?" Lily looked around. She could see boats only as specks in the distance.

"No. I thought you wanted a turn at being the captain."

Lily stuffed her hat in the bag and scrambled

out of the seat. "I sure do." She moved over beside him. "Tell me what to do." She placed her hand on the steering wheel and one on the throttle.

Max chuckled. "I like a woman I don't have to ask twice."

She grinned over her shoulder.

"Okay, all you have to do is push the throttle forward and pull back to slow down. You have to get pretty fast to plane off."

"Are you ready?"

He moved back in the seat. She stood between his legs. "I'm ready."

Lily shoved the throttle and the powerful engine roared as the water rolled. The front end of the boat came up. She slowly gave it more gas. The long hull stood high, making it difficult to see.

Max put his hand over hers and thrust the throttle further forward. "You're going to have to give it more speed to get it to plane out."

The front lowered so she could see the horizon in the distance. Max's hands came to her waist. She liked his steady presence behind her.

As she entered a turn, Max put his hand on the wheel and eased them back into a wider arch. "You can't turn too tightly. We don't want to roll over."

"Aye-aye, Captain."

His hands returned to her waist, and she spent another half an hour enjoying the freedom of the water, wind and weight of Max's hands resting on her. Pulling the throttle toward her, the boat settled in the water.

"That was so much fun." Excitement still ran through her.

Max turned the switch off and the engine quieted. "Are you ready for lunch?"

"We're going to eat all the way out here?" She looked at the ocean surrounding them and the land in the distance.

"Sure, why not?" Max moved her hair away from her neck, kissed it, then nudged her out of the way.

She looked at the sky. "Don't tell me you're having our lunch helicoptered in."

"I didn't think about that, but it would've been impressive."

"Are you trying to impress me?" She studied him a moment.

He looked at her. "You know, I think I might be." Max sounded as surprised as she felt. "But I've messed up with the helicopter. I just had the hotel fix a picnic basket, and I put it and a cooler in when I rented the boat this morning. Not so impressive."

Lily stopped Max with a hand on his arm.

She cupped his face in her fingers and kissed him. "Believe me, I'm impressed. This is the nicest day I can remember spending in a long time. Thank you."

"You're welcome." Max smiled, then pulled up one of the seat cushions on the back bench. He removed a basket and blanket, handing them to her. He set aside another cushion and lifted out a small cooler. Moving around her, he climbed the three small steps between the front seats and stepped over the windshield.

"What're you doing?"

He stood on the hull of the boat. "I'm going to set out our picnic."

"We're eating up there?" Had Max lost his mind?

"We are."

"We won't fall off?" She looked out over the water.

"I don't plan to." He offered his hand. "Give me your hand and I'll help you over."

Lily went up the steps and took his hand. As Max steadied her, she climbed over the shield and found her footing.

"This area up here is plenty big." Max set the basket down and spread out the blanket.

The breeze flipped the edges, and Lily carefully stepped to help him.

"Go ahead and sit on it." Max placed a foot at the corner.

Lily sat, smoothing out the area around her.

Max picked up the cooler and put it aside while he went after the basket. He returned and set it down in the middle of the blanket before he lowered himself beside it.

Lily watched as he removed their lunch. Shrimp cocktail, a tomato salad and crackers. "This looks wonderful."

"I figured you'd had a big breakfast with Ivy and would like something light for lunch."

"This is perfect." He was perfect. And thoughtful.

"Will you open things while I get the drinks?" Max pulled the cooler toward him.

Lily picked up the crackers. As she ate, she looked out over the blue-green water. "Thanks for doing this. It truly is amazing. I would've never dreamed of eating on the front of a boat like this. Or out here on the water."

He grinned. "What about being with me?"

She was grateful for her dark glasses. "Especially that."

Max chuckled.

Lily quickly said, "But I'm glad I am."

"Aw, and she says all the right things. I'm flattered."

Feeling contrite, she touched his arm. "I meant it."

Max kissed her. "I know you do. I'm glad I'm here with you. You didn't tell me how it went with Ivy this morning."

"Fine."

"Did you talk about her running away?" He dipped a shrimp in the sauce.

"She told me what'd happened. I reminded her that I worry about her. She cried. I did too. She promised not to ever do it again."

"Will she keep that promise?"

Max acted relaxed and nonchalant, but she had no doubt he watched and listened carefully. "I believe she will. We talked about voicing our feelings. Asking if she could call me."

He nodded. "Sounds reasonable. What did she get mad about?"

"She wants to work outside the compound at a shoe store. Some of the residents work off the property and she's asked to."

"So why doesn't she?" Max picked up his bowl of salad.

"Because I told the administrator I didn't think it was a good idea. I worry about her getting led astray by someone or taking the wrong bus." She shrugged. "Anything could happen."

"You're probably right." He shrugged. Something in his tone made her think that wasn't all he thought, but the day had been too wonderful for them to fight, so she said no more.

They ate in silence for a while. Lily listened to the lap of the water against the boat and the sound of the seagulls above. Finished with her meal, she lay on the blanket with her hands behind her head and closed her eyes. "What do you see your future like?"

Max whistled. "Wow, you went deep with that question."

"I'm sorry. That's not really any of my business. I was just thinking how often what we think life will be like doesn't end up like that at all."

"You're right about that. Mine hasn't turned out the way I thought."

"How's that?" Suddenly, she wasn't as sleepy as she had been.

"I thought I'd be settled down with a wife and family by now. Even a dog."

She liked listening to his deep, warm voice. "I'm surprised. You have never struck me as the kind of guy who thinks about those sorts of things."

"Just because I like to enjoy life doesn't mean that I don't want those things too. What do you want? Besides to take care of Ivy."

She sighed. How would he react if she told

him? She given up on even thinking about having a man in her life after Jeff. She hadn't thought she could trust another guy. Wasn't sure she could take a chance on Ivy becoming attached to someone who would let them down again. Then came Max. She'd started to dream again. But she needed to put a stop to that. Except Jeff had used her. Max would never do that. "I want that, of course, but I'd like to have a baby."

"What about a husband to go with that baby?"

Was he volunteering? "Sure. I want what my parents had. I want to find someone who I can be happy with."

"I don't think happiness is something we plan for but something that happens. Everyone defines happiness by different guidelines. My father sees it as dollars and cents. You see it as a baby."

"And you?" She opened her eyes just enough to watch his expression.

He leaned back on his palms and crossed his legs at the ankles. He looked like he belonged to the world of fast boats and leisurely afternoons, as if he had no cares in the world. "I was thinking that right now. With you, I'm about as happy as I've ever been."

"Are you trying to sweet-talk me?"

His grin flashed, showing straight white teeth. "Do I need to?"

She placed her hand over her heart. "No woman wants to be thought of as easy."

"There's the Lily that I know so well. I assure you I don't think you're easy. It has taken me years to get to know you. Now I have, I want to know all."

"There's not much to know."

"I'm not sure that's true. Like, have you thought any more about us marketing our product together?"

She closed her eyes again. A trickle of caution ran through her. Was Max just being nice to her because he wanted something? "Is it really that important to you that I agree to packaging Skintec with your glue?"

"I wish I could say no, but yeah, it is. It means a lot to my father. It would make him very happy. But I want you to do what you think is right. That is the most important thing." He sounded encouraging and disappointed at the same time. What was going on between him and his father?

"You sure know how to apply the pressure."

He brushed a strand of hair off her face. "It isn't my intent to make you feel that way. Make the decision that you think you need to. I just wanted to answer you honestly."

She could appreciate that. The only thing about them going into business together is that they would forever be bound. What if something went wrong between them? "We would always be partners."

"Would that be so bad? I thought we had become friends."

For her, what she felt was more than friendship. She should have been more careful. "We have."

"You can trust me. I'll always have your best interests at heart. I never want to hurt you, on a personal level or a business one."

"That's a big promise."

"It is, but I mean it." He leaned over her, covering her lips with his.

Max did mean it. Lily had become too important for him to ever intentionally do anything that would hurt her. He'd been looking for the right woman for a long time, and he believed he'd found her in Lily. He wouldn't ruin what was between them, even for his father.

Her arms came around his neck and he held her tighter. He wanted moments like this one for the rest of his life. His hand slid under her tank top and over her belly to her breasts. Cupping one, he teased it until her nipple stood tight against the thin padding that covered it.

Lily moaned and wiggled against him.

His hand left her breast and traveled over her middle to flip open the button of her shorts. She pulled at his shirt. He leaned away long enough to pull it over his head. Lily wasted no time in moving her hands all over his chest. Taking her lips again, he pushed at her shirt raising it and pushing her bra away until she was bare to his touch. He took a moment to admire her in the sunlight before his mouth covered her nipple and tugged.

Lily arched to meet him as her fingers tunneled through his hair.

He reached around her and unclipped her bra giving him full excess to her breasts. "You're so beautiful."

"Mmm."

The sound of a boat in the distance registered, making him pull back to see if they were going to have company. He didn't see anyone, but he wasn't going to take a chance on them being caught unaware. She would never forgive him if she was put in an embarrassing situation.

"I think we need to take this to a place a little more secluded. I wouldn't want to share you with anyone who happens to come too close." With great effort, he pushed away.

Lily sat up, looking dazed.

Max brushed a finger over her cheek. "I like that look on you. It makes me feel good."

She tugged on her shirt, covering herself.

"Don't get too tidy. Because I don't plan to let you stay that way." He quickly gathered their meal debris and stuffed it in the basket before dropping the container into the passenger seat. He pulled her to her feet and gathered the blanket. Throwing it into the bottom of the boat, he stepped over the windshield and helped her follow.

"Wait here a moment." He let her go, picked up the blanket and spread it out over the floor. He lay down on his side, propped his head on his hand and patted the area next to him. "Join me."

Lily looked at him a moment before she lowered herself to her knees and leaned down to kiss him. She nudged his shoulders back and straddled his hips. His hands found her waist, fingertips gripping her tender skin. Her center moved lower, rubbing over his straining manhood.

Max pulled her shirt and loose bra over her head in seconds.

Lily, in an unexpected show of boldness, offered him her breasts like ripe fruit waiting for just him to enjoy their sweetness. He took her gift and feasted on the beauty above him.

Lily with her head thrown back and the sun blazing behind her heated his blood. He had to have her.

She kneaded his shoulders as his tongue laved her breasts, first one then the other. His hand slid down to her thighs, moving under her shorts until his finger found her center, wet with want.

Her sweet mouth found his. He would have never guessed this hot, wanton woman lived quietly behind that subdued–Dr. Evans veneer. He liked this Lily. A lot.

Teasing her heated opening a moment, he then plunged inside her. She pushed down on his fingers wanting more.

"Take your pants off," she growled as she crawled off him.

As she removed her shorts and panties, he stood to do the same with his clothes. She looked at him with such brashness and admiration his chest swelled. They stood naked to the world as her hand wrapped around him, timid and testing.

To his amazement he grew at her touch. Hadn't he been harder than he'd ever been already? He caressed her hip to her thigh and back.

"I've never seen or felt a man like this. You are, uh, marvelous."

No other man had ever let her enjoy his body? What selfish lovers they all must have been. He grinned. "I'm all yours for as long as you want."

She continued to grip him while stroking his chest. She kissed his shoulder, his neck on her way to his mouth. There she tugged his bottom lip with her teeth.

At this rate, Lily might kill him, but he would die with a smile on his face. He cupped her perfect behind and found her center. She spread her legs, letting him touch her freely. His finger located her special spot and Lily tensed, stopping her movements, and looked at him, eyes wide.

"I want to watch you come for me. I want you to see who's giving you pleasure." He wanted her never to doubt he was the one that could do so like no other.

She twisted and pushed down on his finger. Her gaze never waved from his. A wild look more beautiful than he'd seen ever before filled her eyes.

He pulled from her. She groaned displeasure. After he reached for his pants to pull out a packet he guided her to the blanket. Lily threw her leg over him, straddling him. Her hot center ran the distance of his manhood. It was his turn to groan.

"Lily, if you keep that up, I'm going to be a goner."

"I don't care," she murmured as she moved again, this time more slowly.

"But I want this to be about us, not just me." The truth of that shocked him.

She pressed against him a sassy grin on her lips.

"Stop teasing me, and let me get this on." He held up the square package.

Lily moved back and took the protection from him and slowly rolled it over his length.

"You are trying to be the death of me." He moved to roll her beneath him, but she held steady and slowly slid over him, taking him completely.

Her look of supreme satisfaction filled him with hot desire, but he didn't act on it, preferring to let Lily have her way with him. She gave him painfully sweet pleasure like he'd never had before as she rose so high that she almost lost him before she dipped down to take him into her again with a deep rush.

Unable to stand it any longer, he rose up to meet her, then turned her on her back and plunged hard and fast. Lily's eyes flew open. She looked at him in surprise as her hands bit into his sides and her body shuddered.

She remained suspended a moment before she shook and relaxed. "Oh my goodness."

He gave her a quick kiss, then pumped into her like a desperate man. With a roar, he found a shattering release. He fell to his back beside her and pulled Lily to him.

How could he ever leave her?

CHAPTER EIGHT

LILY COULDN'T BELIEVE how easy and natural it was for her and Max to spend the morning getting ready for work together. It was what she believed it must be like for a settled couple. Hadn't it been the same with her parents? Jeff had never stayed over. In fact, more than once, she'd thought him too eager to leave. Would it always be this right between her and Max?

She feared she'd like it too much. They lived thousands of miles away from each other. What kind of relationship could they have? She needed to think straight. Less like a dreamy-eyed woman who'd just gotten out of bed after heavenly morning sex and more like the practical professional she was.

She looked at Max across her kitchen table. He grinned. "What?"

"Nothing." Her heart whipped into race speed. Just like that, she basked in the warmth of having Max in her life.

That sexy grin she'd come to love spread across his lips. "I wouldn't look at me that way if you don't intend to keep your patients waiting."

"I'd better not." Lily stood and picked up her plate. She grinned down at him. "Even if I might like to."

He caught her by the wrist as she moved by him. He tugged her into his lap. "Being a few minutes late wouldn't be so bad."

She kissed him. "No, not so bad, but I really need to be on time. I'd like to see Mr. Roth before I go to clinic." Reluctantly she stood and continued to the kitchen sink.

"Then, I'll be ready to go in ten minutes."

She had to remind herself life wasn't all fun and games. More often than not, it didn't go the way she wanted it to. Didn't the fact Max was leaving soon prove that? It probably didn't even matter to him. The best she could tell, Max became truly serious only when he was in the operating room.

At the hospital, they went straight to ICU to see Mr. Roth.

"It looks like you're resting well." She looked at her patient's chart. "I'm glad to see it."

"Much better. Except for the new scar," Mr. Roth said.

"It won't be long before you'll be up and

moving around." Max checked out the medicine pump behind Mr. Roth's head.

"Dr. James is right. You should go to the floor this afternoon and be home in a couple of days." Lily smiled at the man.

Mr. Roth gave her a wry smile. "I already feel better."

"That's what I like to hear." Lily handed the nurse the chart.

Mr. Roth looked from her to Max. "I have you and Dr. James to thank for that."

"I just happened to be along. Dr. Evans is a brilliant surgeon," Max assured Mr. Roth.

Lily couldn't deny she liked hearing Max's praise. "Don't let him fool you. Dr. James is the one who saw the spot causing the trouble."

"Either way, I'm glad to have you both there to fix me up," Mr. Roth assured them.

"Glad to do it." She patted him on the shoulder. "See you later this afternoon." Lily walked out of ICU with a feeling of success, and oddly, she didn't mind sharing it with Max.

As they made their way to the clinic building, Lily couldn't believe that Max had been there just over a week. It seemed he'd been in her life forever. Carol, the nurse, was waiting on them when they arrived at her wing of exam rooms.

"I don't think I have a horribly long clinic

today." She glanced at the printed list the nurse handed her.

"I'll have to leave you at ten-thirty. I have a lunch meeting with Dr. Lee."

"What's going on between you two?" This was his and Dr. Lee's second meeting. She walked to the first exam room door and Max followed.

"Is that jealousy I hear?" Matt's eyes narrowed.

"It is not!"

He leaned close and said for her ears only, "I like the idea of you being jealous."

Lily huffed. "You need to get that idea out of your head."

"You're saying you don't care?" He grinned, but his eyes held no humor.

Thankfully, she opened the door to the exam room, giving her an opportunity not to answer. Did she dare share with Max how much she did care? What would happen if she did?

She had seen five of her patients when she glanced at the list to find Mr. Cruz's name next. She liked the man, but he could be too aggressive. Yet he did feed her self-esteem. He still had a difficult time with boundaries.

"What's the story on this next patient?" Max asked, moving around to look over her shoulder.

She handed Max the pad and knocked on the door. "Here, see for yourself."

Max took it.

She entered the room, leaving the door open. "Mr. Cruz, it's good to see you."

The young man, dressed in a sports coat, knit shirt and tan slacks, stood. "I've asked you to call me Miguel, Dr. Evans."

She quirked her mouth to the side and shook her head. "How've you been feeling?"

"Pretty good. That medicine you gave me last time really helped."

"I'm glad to hear it. How about sitting on the exam table for me and letting me have a look at you?"

"Certainly." He glanced at Max, who had just entered.

Lily nodded toward Max. "This is Dr. James. He's visiting with us this week."

"Hello," Max said.

"Hi. You're a lucky man to be hanging out with Dr. Evans. She's the best."

"I can't disagree with that," Max looked down at the pad. "How long have you had hepatitis C?"

"Aw, about ten years. It showed up when I was a senior in high school," Mr. Cruz said, but he watched her carefully as she listened to his heart, then lungs.

"Lay down for me and let me check your liver." She stepped away.

He removed his jacket and shirt then climbed up again putting his back on the cushion table.

Lily had to admit he was fit looking. "Are you still running daily?"

"Yes, but I only go in the early morning when it isn't so hot."

"Smart thing to do. Now, lie still for me and let me push around on you some." She rubbed her hands together, warming them. "They're going to be cold. Sorry."

"Cool hands, warm heart is what I've always heard." Mr. Cruz grinned.

Lily smiled as she pushed on her patient's middle, just below his right ribs. "I wouldn't count on that. Let me know if anything hurts." She felt for the ridge of his liver and around the sides. It was enlarged more than it had been six months earlier.

"I don't like that look on your face, pretty doctor," Mr. Cruz said.

"The disease is progressing. We're going to need to talk about a plan of action sooner rather than later."

As if she had said nothing life changing, Mr. Cruz teased, "Hey, doc. I don't like it when you frown. Put that smile back on your face. You'll figure it out."

Lily sure hoped he was right.

Max cleared his throat. "Do you mind if I examine you?"

Mr. Cruz's attention moved to Max and his demeanor turned more serious. "Sure, I guess."

Max moved in close as she stepped out of his way. Lily watched as Max efficiently palpated the same spot she had.

When he finished, he backed away. "Thanks, Mr. Cruz."

"You can get dressed now," Lily said as she took the pad from Max and typed in her findings. "I'd like to see you back in three months. If you start feeling bad in any way, call me."

Mr. Cruz grinned. "Even if it's for a drink."

She chuckled. "I've already told you that I don't date my patients."

Mr. Cruz shrugged. "You can't blame a guy for trying."

Lily started toward the door. "I'll see you here in *three* months then."

Max entered the hall and closed the door. He hissed, "That man was flirting with you!"

"Ah, he's just teasing. He doesn't mean anything by it. His just one of those South Beach guys living off his father's money. He's harmless."

"Didn't look harmless to me." Max's face was all tight angles and clenched jaw.

Lily studied him a moment, then walked to the next examination room. The warmth of satisfaction rippled through her. She whispered, "Is that jealousy I hear?"

"You're damn right it is," he spat.

She liked feeling wanted by a man who could have anybody he desired. With a spring in her step, she entered the exam room.

Two patients later, Max led her into an empty room and closed the door.

"What's going on?" Puzzlement made her search Max's face.

"I have to leave, and I didn't want to do it until I've kissed you."

If he was looking for a way to make her puddle at his feet with a sigh of contentment, that had been the thing to say.

Max took her into his arms and gave her a kiss that had her clinging to him. He stepped back, his breath ragged. "I think that's enough in a public place and with you still having patients to see." He walked to the door. "Why don't I take you to dinner tonight?"

She missed his warmth already. Her mouth tightened in disappointment. "I'm sorry. Fridays are when Ivy comes to the house and spends the night."

"Chicken strips and tater tots are on the menu, then?"

She grinned. "Actually, she asked for spaghetti and meatballs tonight."

"That's one of my favorites."

Was Max fishing for an invitation? "Would you like to join us for dinner?"

He quickly said, "I thought you'd never ask."

She laughed. "You really do get excited about spaghetti and meatballs."

"I'm sure I'll enjoy the food, but the dinner company is what I'm really interested in." He took a step toward her.

Sadness washed through her. "You can't spend the night. Ivy wouldn't understand. I don't want to confuse her."

He nodded. "I understand. But I don't have to like it."

What Lily didn't say was that she didn't want Ivy to become invested in Max if he wouldn't be around permanently. The chances for that happening weren't great. She rarely included Ivy in her relationships, but Lily had so little time left with Max, she didn't want to give up any more than she had to.

"Call me when you're finished meeting with Dr. Lee, and hopefully, I'll be done with rounds. We'll head home."

"I'm looking forward to that part." Max gave her a quick kiss and opened the door.

* * *

Max waited only long enough to put the two bags of groceries he held down on Lily's kitchen table before he took her in his arms and kissed her soundly.

"What's that all about?" Lily watched him with bright eyes.

"I've missed you."

"We've been together the last hour."

"Yeah, but I didn't have a chance to kiss you and I missed doing so." He'd found himself thinking about her the entire time he was meeting with Dr. Lee.

Lily rewarded him with smile. Yes, he could stand having that expression in his life every day. Lily was looking at him like he was her favorite candy.

After they left the hospital, they had stopped by a bodega to pick up some items Lily needed for the evening meal. He had followed her around the small store, holding a basket while she placed pasta and vegetables into it. He couldn't remember the last time he'd done something so domestic. It must have been when he was very small, because for most of his life a cook had prepared the family meals. What made the activity particularly interesting was he'd enjoyed every minute of his and Lily's shopping stop.

Lily seemed as meticulous about buying her groceries as she was about everything else she did. He smiled when she picked up a brownie mix box and placed it in the basket. "I think I'd like to have these for dessert tonight. Maybe à la mode."

Max liked her mischievous grin. "That sounds good."

"Men like ice cream, I understand." She looked over her shoulder at him.

"I don't know about other men, but I do." He stepped close to her. "I like other things too."

Lily rewarded him with a blush and a shy smile. "Behave."

He liked teasing her. She always gave him such an enticing reaction. As if other men in her life had never done so.

Lily nudged him away, then stepped to the kitchen counter and began unloading one of the bags. "I need some space. I have to get the sauce started before I leave to get Ivy."

"I can do that for you, if you think Ivy wouldn't mind."

Lily stopped midmovement and looked at him. "Are you sure?"

"I wouldn't volunteer if I wasn't."

Lily didn't say anything for a moment, still watching him with a mixture of amazement and concern. Finally, she responded, "I'll call and ask her. She does know you, but I've never had anyone else pick her up."

"Why not?" Had her boyfriend never had any interaction with the sister Lily was so devoted to?

"Mostly because they never asked to."

Her ex must have been as self-centered as Max had gathered.

"Let me call. I'd need to do so anyway to let them know someone else is coming to get her."

Lily quickly spoke to Ivy. A smile reached her eyes after whatever Ivy said. Seconds later, Lily spoke to someone else, telling them Max would be by to get Ivy before she ended the conversation.

"I guess it was okay with Ivy."

Lily nodded. "Better than okay with her. It seems you've charmed another Evans woman."

Max pulled her to him. "Maybe so, but I'm only interested in kissing the one in my arms." His lips found hers.

It took Max thirty minutes in light traffic to get to where Ivy lived. He shouldn't have been surprised at the lovely place with its more decorative-than-restrictive gate and stucco walls. He requested entrance through a speaker. Soon, he drove along a circular drive, around a green manicured yard with groupings of furniture under low trees. He pulled in front of a low white building with lush plants and landscaping. If he hadn't known better, he would have believed it was an exclusive country club or retirement center.

Lily must pay a great deal for Ivy to live there.

He parked beneath a portico. Sitting in one of the rocking chairs nearby was Ivy. She wore a big smile as she jumped up and waved at him. "Hi, Max."

"Hello, Ivy. It's nice to see you again."

"I'm ready to go." She picked up a bag near one of the large wooden double doors that were the entrance to the place.

"Shouldn't we go inside and let somebody know you're leaving?"

She thought for a moment. "Yeah, I'll do that."

"I think that's the smart thing to see to all the time. You don't want anyone to have to worry about you."

Her face darkened. "I made Lily worry."

Max patted her shoulder. "I know, but it's all right now. The thing is to try not to do it again."

Ivy's face brightened. "I won't. I'll talk to someone about my feelings."

Max grinned. "That would be the right idea. Now, let's go tell someone you're leaving. Lily has spaghetti waiting for us."

"It's one of my favorites."

"Mine too." Matt opened one of the doors for her.

Minutes later, they were back at the car. Matt picked up Ivy's bag and placed it in the trunk.

"Can we ride with the top down?" Ivy asked.

"Sure, it's a nice afternoon." He pushed the button to lower the covering.

Ivy watched in rapt attention as the top slowly folded behind the back seat. By the time it settled, she had scrambled into the front.

Max scooted behind the driving wheel. "Buckle up."

Ivy did as she was told without question, then started talking and asking questions without pause. Max patiently answered them and, a number of times, chuckled at her reaction.

They were almost to Lily's house when Ivy's voice turned serious. "You like my sister, don't you?"

"Yes, of course I do." He smiled at her. "I like you too."

"I mean *like* like her."

A traffic light ahead had turned red, and he waited until he'd stopped before answering. His look met Ivy's. "Yes, I *like* like your sister."

"You kiss her?"

"I like kissing her very much." This interview made him almost as uncomfortable as the one he'd had with his first date's father. He had the distinct feeling his and Lily's relationship hung on how well he answered Ivy's questions.

"Jeff made her cry. He didn't like me."

"I promise not to make Lily cry." Max made sure to look Ivy in the eyes.

"Good." She nodded her head. "I like you."

Max chuckled. That might have been the highest praise he'd ever received. "I like you too."

As soon as he pulled into the driveway, the back door opened and Lily came to meet them as if she had been watching eagerly for them. She wore a large smile. It hit him in the chest just how much he did care for Lily. Somehow, she made the world brighter for him. He'd never thought he'd feel this way about anyone. This is what it felt like, being enough for someone. To measure up, to have them be proud of you for just being you. The feeling had eluded him until Lily came along. Wasn't this sense of belonging what he'd been looking for all his adult life? To arrive home to a greeting from Lily every day would be an amazing gift. It would be something he'd never take for granted.

Lily looked between him and Ivy.

Max gave her a reassuring smile.

Ivy popped out of the car and went to Lily. "Max put the top down. It was so much fun. He told me to buckle."

Lily gave her an indulgent grin, then a hug. "I'm glad to see you."

It crossed his mind that Lily would make a good mother. He'd never thought about a woman he was interested in being in that role. That was one of Lily's greatest attributes, she truly cared about people.

"Come on inside. Supper is almost ready." Lily started toward the back door. Once in the kitchen, she said, "Ivy, why don't you put your bag in your room." As soon as Ivy was out of hearing distance, Lily turned to him. "How did it go?"

"Just fine."

Lily's face softened and she gave him an adoring look. "Thank you for being so nice to my sister. I've never seen her look happier."

"I don't find it hard to spend time with her."

Lily kissed him on the cheek. "You're a special guy."

Max reached for her and pulled her close. "I like that you think so." He gave her a tender kiss.

The rest of the evening was spent talking and laughing over dinner.

They were almost finished when Max said,

"You know the one thing I haven't seen while I've been down here is an alligator. I've never been to the Everglades."

"I would like to see an alligator," Ivy said with enthusiasm.

"I tell you what. I saw a tourist pamphlet about an airboat at the hotel. We could go tomorrow morning."

"Can we?" Ivy looked at Lily with a pleading expression.

Lily's gaze met his. "I don't know. We have the awards banquet tomorrow night."

"We'll go early in the morning." He looked from Lily to Ivy and back. "We should have plenty of time. What do you say?"

"Please," Ivy pleaded to Lily.

"I guess we could do that." Lily didn't sound all that enthusiastic about the idea.

Max reached for her hand and squeezed it. "Come on. It'll be fun."

Lily's eyes narrowed. "How about safe?"

"It'll be safe. Think of it as an adventure."

She shrugged. "Okay."

They cleaned the kitchen and watched a movie of Ivy's choice. Max sat next to Lily on the sofa with his arm lying along the back of the sofa. He resisted pulling her closer, sensing she didn't want too much affection between them in front of Ivy. When the show was over, Lily sent Ivy to bed.

"I'm sorry you can't stay." Lily placed her arm around his waist and leaned into him as they strolled to his car, sitting behind hers in the drive.

Max put his back to the vehicle and brought her to stand between his legs. "Hey, don't worry about it. I understand. Ivy needs time to adjust to us."

"Thanks for understanding. I'll miss you." Lily wrapped her arms around his neck.

Max covered Lily's mouth with his and pulled her tight against him. She opened for him, and his tongue met hers in a dance he wished they were doing in her bedroom behind a closed door. His palms cupped her butt and brought her against his thickened manhood.

At Lily's groan, he nudged her away. He leaned his forehead against hers as he worked to settle his heavy breathing and get his desire under control. "Honey, we keep that up, and we'll be putting on a show for your neighbors."

She giggled.

Placing his hands on her upper arms, he directed her backward far enough he could open the driver's door. He slipped inside, started the car. Before closing the door, he said, "I'll miss holding you tonight."

* * *

Once again, because of Max's urging, Lily found herself stepping out where she never would've gone at all. Getting on an airboat and skimming across the top of swamp water was far beyond her adventure level. She'd lived in the Miami area her entire life, but had never been out into the Everglades. At least sitting on an airboat, she'd be more than three inches out of the water unlike some other tours.

Nothing about the Everglades particularly fascinated her. She knew people who thought the swamp was a wonderfully amazing place, with the animals and plants that were found nowhere else in the worlds. For her, the area always held a bit of terror. Snakes in the water and alligators that could eat her held no allure.

Ivy had been beside herself in anticipation since she'd woken. Lily wasn't feeling as happy or rested. She'd had a difficult time settling into sleep. She wanted to blame it on excitement over the award, to the warm weather and any number of other things running through her head, but what it came down to was she missed having Max next to her. How quickly she'd become dependent on him.

She and Ivy were dressed in T-shirts, long, thin pants and tennis shoes. Lily knew enough to prepare for mosquitos. They didn't need to return with bites all over them. Thankfully when Max arrived, he was dressed similar to them. Ivy ran to greet him while Lily picked up the bag she'd stuffed with sunscreen, hats and a few snacks.

Ivy settled into the back seat. Max gave Lily a quick kiss before he held the door for her to get in. On the hour drive to the border of Everglades National Park, Max and Ivy chatted about the alligators and snakes they hoped to see that day. Lily sat quietly and listened.

Occasionally, she glanced at Max. He would give her a reassuring smile and then return his focus back to the road or to whatever question Ivy had asked. Lily couldn't help but admire his patience and the attention he gave Ivy. Few of the men she had dated ever gave Ivy more than cursory hello. It was nice to hear the delight in her sister's voice.

Max pulled off the main road onto a dirt one. They traveled a short distance before they pulled into an open area with a small metal building. Tall cypress trees with masses of moss hanging from the limbs stood in the swamp behind it. An airboat was secured to the pier nearby. Max brought the car to a stop beside a battered truck.

As they stepped out of the car, a man exited

the building and came to meet them. "Are you Max James?"

"Yes." The men shook hands. Max then introduced her and Ivy.

Hank, with a heavy beard, wearing a T-shirt that read Bite an Alligator Before He Bites You and well-worn cargo pants, looked intimidating until he smiled and spoke. He had a warm voice. "Are we ready to take a ride today?"

"Are we going on that boat?" Ivy pointed to the airboat.

"We sure are. Come on. I'll show you where to sit. Maybe you'd like to drive some today?"

Ivy looked at Lily. "Can I?"

Lily gave her a reassuring smile. "We'll see."

Hank led them down to the pier, built over the standing water. "Before we get on the boat, I need to go over a few rules. Number one, you must wear a life jacket. Two, I need you to remain seated at all times and, three, no hands outside of the boat. I don't want any alligators to be having lunch on us."

Lily shuddered.

She could do this. It would be for only a few hours. Ivy and Max were looking forward to it.

Hank stepped into the boat and helped Ivy to one of the four seats in the front. Ivy sat down.

Max stepped in the craft and helped Lily in.

She took the seat next to Ivy, and Max settled in the one next to her.

"Your life jackets are under your seat," Hank said from behind them. "Put them on and then buckle yourselves in."

Lily got into her jacket, checked Ivy's, then she made sure Ivy's seat belt was secure and snapped hers on.

"All set?" Hank called from where he sat in a high seat behind them.

Max nodded. To her, he said, "You okay?"

Lily glanced at Ivy who had a smile and a look of excitement on her face. One like Lily hadn't seen in a long time. She gripped the edge of the seat and gave Max a nod. "Yeah, I'm sure I am."

The boat's huge fan roared to life. Lily jumped. Max removed her hand from the seat and held it resting on his thigh. Her heart settled with his reassurance.

Ivy looked at her. "This is going to be so much fun."

Soon the boat rocked, and the water rippled around them as Hank used the long-handled stick to put the boat in gear, then another to move the large wind rudders, sending them out into the water.

"Ivy, hang on," Lily called over the noise of the motor.

Despite her insecurities, Lily forgot them some as she looked at the intriguing landscape. The glimmer of the sun off the water on the beautiful cloudless sky. The tall grass blowing in the breeze held her attention. Birds flew as they moved across the water.

"How you doing?" Max asked, his lips close to her ear so he could be heard.

She nodded.

He squeezed her hand.

Ivy sat forward in her seat, her face in the wind.

Hank slowed the boat and cut the engine. They glided into a small glade of water. Before them lay a sea of white birds. Lily had never seen anything like it. Or more beautiful.

Ivy started to say something. Lily placed her hand on her leg. "Shh."

They floated without a noise, watching the amazing scene. At a squawk from one of the birds, they all took flight, creating an even more astonishing sight. Minutes later, the noise of flapping wings and screaming bird-calls moved into the distance.

Hank said, "I thought you might like this. You have to be here at the right time of day to catch the sight. Y'all were lucky."

"That was a lot of birds." Ivy looked at the sky in wonder.

Max chuckled. "That was an understatement."

"Beautiful," Lily murmured.

Hank started the engine once more, and they moved out into a different channel. They traveled up it until they had entered a wide lake. He turned off the boat.

"I wanted to tell you a little bit about the Everglades. There are a million-and-a-half acres of this swampland. It's really a large river. It starts with the Kissimmee River up in the middle of the state. The river dumps into Lake Okeechobee. The swamp is created by the overflow and creates a slow-moving river, which is all this water you see. It's sixty miles wide and a hundred miles long on its way to the ocean.

"There's no other ecosystem like it anywhere else in the world. Mangroves grow here, and there are pine flatwoods. Of course, the best known tree is the cypress tree with the knees sticking up everywhere and their tangle of roots.

"A number of endangered animals live here, like the leatherback turtle, the Florida panther and the manatee. Ivy, don't put your hand in the water."

Lily's head jerked to Ivy. "In your lap, Ivy." She clasped her hands in front of her.

Hank continued, "You don't ever know

what's in the water and if they're hungry. Now we're going to see if we can find one of those endangered species, the American alligator."

Lily flinched. Max gave her hand a squeeze of encouragement.

Hank restarted the boat, and they headed across the lake. Too soon for Lily, they slowed and eased into a narrow channel and under trees. A flop and splash of water draw their attention.

Lily saw the tail of an alligator disappear beneath the water.

"Oh," Ivy whispered.

As they continued to watch, another three alligators slid down the low, dirt bank. The water frothed just off to the right side of the boat.

"We can't sit here, because they'll start bumping the boat. We'll go on down. Watch the banks, and you may catch sight of some baby gators." Hank unhurriedly moved forward.

"Ivy, stay still," Lily reminded her.

"I am. They're scary." Ivy didn't take her eyes off the water.

"There's a baby alligator." Max pointed off to the left.

Ivy, with her voice full of excitement, leaned against Lily. "I see it."

"Let's count them, Ivy," Max suggested. "One, two, three…"

Fifteen minutes later, they came out into open water again.

"We counted twenty-three," Max announced.

"That's a lot," Ivy said with wide eyes.

It was plenty for Lily.

"Yeah, it is," Max agreed.

Hank increased the speed, and all talking stopped. Twenty minutes later, they entered a channel with low-hanging trees filled with moss that blocked out most of the sunlight. Hank announced, "Here is where you need to look for snakes. Pay attention to the low-hanging limbs. They'll be resting on them this time of day."

Lily was absolutely not interested in finding or looking for a snake. Somehow, it seemed to entertain Ivy and Max far more. They treated it like an Easter egg hunt. As they talked and pointed, she focused on the water ahead, hoping they'd soon be out in the open again.

Max looked at her, and his face turned serious. "Hank, I think it's time we head back."

"We have one more stop." The boatman continued at the same speed.

"Please take us in." Max used his firm OR tone.

At Max's stern statement, Hank turned the boat in a wide arc and headed into the sun.

* * *

Max had been so busy trying to give Ivy a good time and letting Lily see that he accepted her sister that he'd failed to give Lily the attention she deserved. When he'd glanced at Lily to find her wearing a sick, fearful look, he'd known he'd messed up. She'd been being strong to give him and Ivy some enjoyment. Once again, she'd sacrificed herself for others. Lily did that too much.

As they rounded a bend in the channel, Max looked ahead to see another airboat floating on the water. A man's head came up, and he waved his arm at them.

Hank eased back on the speed. They came to an idle beside the boat.

It was then that Max could see the man holding his bloody forearm.

"Help me," the man called.

Max released his belt and braced his feet. "Hold it steady, Hank, so I can get to him. I'm a doctor." He reached for the side.

Behind him Lily said to Ivy. "Stay put and don't unbuckle. Keep your hands in. Hank, where's your first aid kit?"

Max thought better of stepping into the other boat, in fear that the two would move away from each other and leave him in the water. Instead, he went down on his hands and knees and crawled across, rolling into the bottom of the other airboat. Hank turned off the motor. It was eerily quiet around them after the roar of the big engine.

"What happened?" Max asked the boatman.

"My arm got caught in the fan."

Max climbed over the metal bench seats. "When did this happen?"

"Just before you came up."

"Lily, I'm going to need something for a tourniquet," Max said over his shoulder. He had no doubt Lily was busy thinking through the problem, as well. The man had turned pale. "And a blanket. Something to treat for shock."

Max could barely make out the mangled muscle and bone for all the blood. The craft bobbed, and he looked behind him to see Lily scrambling toward him. "You should've stayed on the other boat."

"You might need my help." Lily handed him a one-inch strap. "Use this for the tourniquet."

Max took it from her and wrapped it around the man's bicep. Pulling it tight, he watched as the flow of blood slowed. Done, he looked at the man, only to find he had passed out, which was probably the best thing for him. He must be in a great deal of pain.

Lily came up beside him. "We need to get this man in the bottom of the boat so we can get his feet above his heart, then we can see about his arm."

Max nodded. "Agreed. I'll get his shoulders and you take his legs."

Working together, they scooted the man into position. Lily rested his feet on the edge of the boat and efficiently laid an oily beach towel over him along with a couple of life preservers lying nearby.

Max returned his attention to the wound. It needed support and a covering to keep it clean. "Hank, call 9-1-1 and have an ambulance waiting for us. Also, we need a board, stick or something long and steady to secure this arm. Do you have a knife on you?"

"There should be a paddle in the boat somewhere. Here's my knife." Hank started to throw it.

"No, don't do that. We can't afford to lose it in the water," Max called to him.

"I'll get it." Lily scrambled to the front of the boat.

As she started back toward Max, the boat rocked from something bumping it. It happened again.

"The gators smell the blood." Hank's voice carried behind Max.

"Ivy," Lily yelled, fear filling her voice, "I want you to scoot—do not stand, scoot—over one seat to the middle of the boat. Hank, please see she does so and buckles up again. Keep your hands in your lap."

"I'll see she stays safe," Hank's gruff voice assured her.

Another thump against one of the boats reminded Max of how much more serious the situation had become. He pulled his T-shirt off.

Lily stayed low as she worked herself back toward him. She handed him the knife. "I'll get some vitals."

Max nodded and started cutting up his T-shirt into strips. "Before we start securing the arm, let the tourniquet go for a second. His fingers are turning blue."

She did as he requested. By the time she was finished, he had the strips of cloth ready to go.

Another bump rocked the boat from beneath.

Max looked around for a toolbox, spying one under the driver's seat. Stepping over the man, while being careful to hold on to the bar of the seat so he'd not get thrown out, he reached for the case. The last thing they needed was for him to go swimming with the alligators.

"Careful." Lily's hand gripped his pants leg.

He picked up the box, then quickly sat it down. The next nudge of the boat came harder and with a splash of water. Opening the toolbox, he located a screwdriver and went to work on the throttle stick in front of them. "Let's get this done and get out of here."

With the stick removed, he placed it under the man's arm. Max held the limb up and in place while Lily quickly and efficiently wrapped the T-shirt material around it.

The boat shook the next time, enough that water sloshed over the side.

Max called over his shoulder. "Hank, we're ready to get out of here."

"We need to tie up side by side. I can't pull you because of the fan." Hank handed Max some rope. "We have to loop around the cleat at the front of the boat and then at the frame of the fan."

"Will do." Max took the rope Hank pitched him.

He and Hank worked to pull the boats together. The thrashing in the water made the maneuvering difficult. After a couple of false starts, they managed to get them into position.

"I'll tie the back if you'll get the front," Max called to Hank.

Working his way to the driver's seat, he had to lean over to reach the bar he needed. It required he place his foot on the edge of the boat to keep his balance. His foot slipped. He straddled the side. Using all his upper body strength, he pulled his body upward.

Lily's gasp made him look down. An alligator's nose rose out of the water, just below him. Water spilled in. Her arms wrapped his waist, Lily leaned to the side, pulling him back with her bringing his leg out of the water. The boat steadied. Lily released him. He scrambled off her and searched the surface. Seeing nothing, he moved as fast and safely as he could to tie them off to the other boat.

With relief, he called to Hank. "Let's go."

"This will have to be slow and easy," Hank returned.

"Understood."

The motor started, and there was no more talking. Max took a seat next to Lily giving her a hug to show his gratitude. She returned it with tears in her eyes. He wished they could stay like that for a long time, but they had a patient to see to. They turned to check on him. Twice during the trip, he released the tourniquet while Lily did vitals. It took them three times longer to return than it had to come out.

The fellow woke when they were within eyesight of the pier. Lily reassured him. He settled again, a white line of pain around his lips. An ambulance waited in the parking lot. Max gladly handed over the care of the man to the

EMTs. He gave a report about what happened and what he had done, and Lily told them about the man's vitals.

He stood beside Lily, watching as the ambulance pulled away. "This wasn't how I planned the day to go."

Lily placed a hand on his arm. "Hey, this wasn't your fault."

"Some of it was. You hated most of the trip, and then we had an emergency."

She faced him. "It wasn't all bad. I had a new experience to talk about. Some excitement in my life. And Ivy had a ball."

He shrugged. "She did. But I didn't want it to be at your expense."

"I had some time to think on the way back. We make a good team. In an emergency. In the OR. I think our products would make good teammates, as well."

"Are you sure? I don't want you to feel pressured." His father would have his way. This time, with Max's help. At least for once, he had a chance to please him.

She smiled. "I'm sure. Let's go get Ivy. I have an award banquet to attend."

CHAPTER NINE

LILY TWISTED AND turned in front of the mirror attached to her bedroom door. A sense of satisfaction flooded her. She looked her best.

She hadn't originally bought a new dress for the award ceremony, only planning to wear one of her nicest that evening. Instead, she'd splurged on an outfit from a boutique near her house. Time had been tight, but she'd worked it in. She and Max had dropped Ivy off at her place before he took Lily home. After she cleaned up, she'd hurried out on her shopping trip.

Twisting one way, then the other, she checked every angle in the long mirror. The knee-length blush dress swung around her legs. Its color matched the tint of her cheeks and nose where the sun had touched them.

She glowed like she couldn't remember ever doing. Normally, she didn't look forward to awards ceremonies. She tended to remain out of the spotlight. With the anticipation of Max being her escort, excitement hummed through her. How easily Max had become such a central part of her life. She refused to think about him having to leave the next day. They hadn't talked about the future, but she was sure there would be one for them.

She couldn't believe how shameless she'd become where Max was concerned. It was completely unlike her. What was happening to her? Lily grinned. She was in love. Life had become more exciting with Max around. She'd come out of a shell she'd had no idea she'd been living in. The trip to the Everglades hadn't been her favorite outing, but she was super proud of herself for making it. Even more for helping Max. Saving a man's life had been rewarding. She felt alive. Happy.

When was the last time she could have said that?

All because of Max. What was she going to do when he left? Would she go back to living a dull, scared life once again? No, she wouldn't return to that person.

Her focus returned to filling her small clutch purse and putting her heeled shoes on. Max would be there in ten minutes to pick her up for the cocktail party before the banquet.

At the ring of the front doorbell, she hurried

to open it. Max stood there, appearing more dapper than any man had the right to look or a woman's heart could stand. Lily couldn't believe he would be escorting her. Dressed in a blue dress shirt with the collar open, a navy sports jacket over it and cream-colored slacks, he looked like a model straight off a magazine cover. Max truly took her breath away.

Finally, she uttered, "Hey."

"Hi, beautiful. Don't you look lovely?" He studied her from head to toe. His arm slipped around her waist, pulling her close before his lips found hers. The tender kiss made her toes curl and her center heat.

Against her ear he murmured, "Why don't we just forget the cocktail party. Stay here and have our own celebration."

Lily giggled. "I think we'd be missed."

"How about we show up just in time to receive our awards and keep walking afterwards?"

She swatted his arm. "I don't think that would be good for either one of our careers."

"Maybe not, but I want you to know I'm going to spend the entire time thinking about how slowly I'm going to take that dress off you when we get home."

A honeyed warmth washed through her.

She lowered her lashes. "If you go and behave, maybe I'll let you do that."

A sexy gleam filled his eyes and he held up three fingers. "I promise."

Max insisted they take his car. "I want this evening to be like a real date. Me driving you. You holding my hand."

Lily like that idea.

Max opened the car door for her and waited until she settled before going around and taking the driver's seat. "I'll put the top down on our way back. I'm sure you don't want to mess up your hair while getting there."

"I'd appreciate that." She patted her hair. "I did put some time into it."

As Max drove, he commented, "You really are beautiful. But especially tonight."

She took his hand and held it. "Thank you."

"You got a touch of sun today. I really do love the weather here." Max looked at her and smiled, giving her hand a squeeze. "New York can be so brutal during the winter months. It overshadows the rest of the year."

Would he consider relocating in Florida, and then they could really see where this relationship could go? "You ever think about moving your practice elsewhere?"

"Occasionally, I do."

"Life's too short to be unhappy where you

are." Wasn't that something she'd just recently learned?

Max glanced at her. "Have you ever thought about going elsewhere?"

"No, I like the hospital, and Miami is a good place to live. Ivy is happy here, as well. I see myself growing old here."

He nodded. "I think this city suits you. And I can understand about Ivy."

"By the way, you were great with her today. I appreciate that."

Max glanced at her. "You act like that's a hardship. It isn't."

"Others have found it to be."

"That's on them." His thumb caressed the top of her hand. "I hadn't planned on us having such an exciting morning. I hope you got some rest this afternoon."

"Not exactly. I actually went out to buy this dress."

His hand released hers and he brushed it over her knee, leaving it there. "You made a nice choice. You look amazing. The other men are going to be jealous that you're with me."

Lily giggled. "Thanks. I'm not sure about that."

"I am." His emphatic tone made her heart expand.

"I'm positive the women won't be able to

keep their eyes off you. They already have trouble doing that anyway."

"I don't care about what any woman thinks except the one who doesn't become crazy at the sight of blood, is devoted to her sister and kisses like there is no tomorrow." He rubbed his thumb along the side of her knee.

"See, there you go, being Mr. Charming. I wouldn't be much of a doctor if I couldn't stand a little blood."

He chuckled. When they stopped in traffic, he turned to look at her. "You have a problem with me being charming."

"No, I just have a problem with being part of a pack. I'd like to stand out among the crowd."

"Honey, you have no need to worry. You're special in general and to me in particular. In many ways." He squeezed her knee. "I'll be glad to prove that to you as soon as we get back your place."

If Max's fingers continued to caress her, she'd soon be telling him to turn around and take her home. She reached for his hand and brought it to her lap.

Half an hour later, she walked beside Max, her hand in his, as they entered the ultramodern hotel in downtown Miami. They were directed to the ballroom down a long glass-and-shiny-metal hallway. The setting sun created prisms of light around them. It made her think of being in a kaleidoscope. She sighed.

Max lightly squeezed her hand. "You okay?"

"Better than okay."

He gave her a sexy smile and a wink.

Heat washed through her. She stood a little taller, being with Max. His reaction to her appearance had her feeling like the luckiest woman in the world. With Jeff, she'd always felt like she didn't measure up. In hindsight, she couldn't figure out what she'd seen in him. The one part of his nature that stood out the most was his selfishness. Next to Max's personality, it was a glaring character flaw.

As they approached the people mingling around a high table over drinks, Max let go of her hand and placed his at the small of her back. The possessive action boosted her confidence. She was a winner tonight in more ways than one.

He leaned down and spoke into her ear. "I bet no one here would ever guess, that just hours ago, we were fighting off alligators and trying to save a man's arm."

"I wouldn't. I wonder how he's doing." She couldn't believe she'd gotten so caught up in herself that she hadn't called to check on the man.

"He was in surgery when I phoned. They think they can save his arm."

She placed her hand on his chest for a moment. "That's good to hear."

A short, squat man with thinning hair headed their direction with his hands outstretched. "Dr. James and Dr. Evans. It's so good to see you. I'm Dr. Molasky."

Lily recognized his name as the director of the awards ceremony.

"I'm glad to be here." Max shook the man's hand and passed her a sly glance.

She kept her features even, though she thought of what Max had said about he'd rather be taking her dress off. "Hi. I'm looking forward to the evening."

Dr. Molasky shook her hand, as well. "Please enjoy the cocktails. In a few minutes, we'll move into the ballroom. Your seats are at one of the tables up front."

"Thank you." Lily gave the nervous-looking man a reassuring smile.

As Dr. Molasky walked away, Max asked, "May I get you a drink?"

"I'll have some white wine, please." She needed something to settle her nerves.

Max's lips brushed her temple. "I'll be right back."

While he was gone, a number of her colleagues and people in her field approached her to say congratulations.

Max returned and joined the group. He handed her a glass, and his hand came to rest at her waist again. Obviously, Max didn't mind letting everyone know they were a couple. She wasn't sure how she felt about it, given his reputation and the fact they hadn't talked about the future. But she refused to let that ruin her evening.

"Maxwell," a woman called from behind them.

Max turned and she did, as well.

"Mom. Dad. You didn't tell me you were going to be here."

Lily had just gotten used to the idea of her and Max, and now she'd be meeting his parents. This, she would have preferred to have prepared for. She bravely raised her chin as Max excused them from the group and ushered her over to the older couple.

Max looked remarkably like his father, but there was a hardness to him that Max didn't have. Max had inherited his mother's eyes and smile. Petite, with a fashion forward hairstyle, Mrs. James's razor-sharp look told Lily she missed little.

Right at that moment, Mrs. James seemed to be summing up Lily and the way her son's hand touched her back. Lily decided she must have passed the test when the woman blinked and her smile widened.

Max handed his drink to Lily as he wrapped his mother in a tight hug. He shook hands with his father and patted his back in true male style, but it didn't look as affectionate between them as it should have. A tenseness vibrated off Max, as if he wasn't completely comfortable around his father.

Max put his hand at her back again and had her take a step forward. "Mom, Dad, this is Dr. Lily Evans."

"It's nice to meet you," Mrs. James said with sincerity while curiosity rang in her voice.

"Dr. Evans? You're the doctor who created Skintec." Mr. James didn't sound as if he was making pleasant conversation.

"I didn't know you two were going to be here," Max said before she and Mr. James could continue their conversation.

"Do you think I'd miss my brilliant son's achievement?" Mrs. James sounded like a proud mother of a child in preschool who was receiving his first award.

Lily thought it was sweet. It made her miss her own parents. They would be proud of her.

"The James Company is a major sponsor of

the event. It's good PR for the company for me to make an appearance."

Lily winced for Max at his father's callous statement, but Max seemed unaffected.

"I realize that, but you usually send a representative to these sorts of events." Max's voice remained level as if this was a normal conversation between the two men, with no feelings involved.

"Max," his mother took his arm, "of course, your father wanted to be here for you, as well. This is a well-earned award."

Lily watched as Max plastered on a smile that didn't reach his eyes.

His father added, "Of course, I did. You and Dr. Evans have both created wonderful products."

"Thank you," Lily said.

"I understand from my boy he has convinced you to package Skintec with Vseal."

Max had already told his father she'd agreed, when she'd done so only earlier this afternoon? Had Max been that sure of her going along with what he wanted?

Mr. James slapped Max on the shoulder. "I knew when I sent you down here you'd be able to get her to agree."

Her stomach lurched. The feeling of being ill washed over her. She'd been used. Again.

"Dad…" Max looked at her. His eyes begged for her to let him explain.

Lily swallowed hard. Had Max wanted to be a part of her team to get close to her? Had he pretended to like Ivy? Worse, had he taken her to bed to seal the deal? She looked around. Anywhere but at Max. She wanted to run, but she had to get through this evening somehow.

Mr. James continued to talk, completely unaware of the drama between her and Max. "I've been asked to say a few words. Tonight would be a great time to announce this partnership and the fact The James Company will be the packaging outlet."

The doors to the ballroom opened.

"We should go in," Max stated in a tight voice.

Lily placed their glasses on a nearby table and headed toward the entrance.

Max remained beside her as they made their way to the front of the room. She found the place card with her name on it. Max wasn't sitting beside her, and he deftly moved people around until he was next to her. His parents, not surprisingly, were seated at the same table. Max's mother's chair was next to her son, with his father on her other side.

Lily sat stiffly in her seat, wishing she could gracefully get out of the evening. This was the second time she'd been humiliated where Max was concerned. Why had she let herself believe? In him? What she'd hoped for? In happiness?

She knew who Max was. He was a player. She should have known he didn't really care for her. What made her think he would pick her out of all the women he could have? Once again, she'd acted like a love-struck idiot. He'd used her. Why was she so gullible?

It hadn't taken anything but that one statement from Max's father to squash her happiness. Somehow, the evening had taken on a different feel. One of betrayal.

Max had to fix this. What had his father been thinking? Only about himself. The look on Lily's face the moment she'd seen him again in the OR had returned. He could well imagine what she had running through her head. That she'd misjudged another man. That he had used her just as her ex had. In her mind, he was no better than Jeff. That was the last thing he wanted her to believe. It was the furthest thing from the truth. He had to convince Lily of that. He hadn't taken her to bed to get something from her. More important, he hadn't acted like Ivy's friend to get to Lily.

Somehow, he had to prove that to Lily.

The cool wind coming from Lily's direction made him shiver. It wasn't going to be easy. He put his arm around the back of her chair, blocking their conversation from others. She stiffened. "It isn't like it sounded. Give me a chance to explain."

Several people came up to congratulate them, ending any conversation that he and Lily might have. He'd have to settle for later. He feared that would be too late.

Their table filled. The servers went to work bringing them food. All the while, Max remained aware of Lily beside him. All the bloom had left her cheeks. This should be a big night for them both, and his father's greed and Max's desire to please had destroyed it. Max had never felt so low or inadequate.

Lily said all the right things to those joining them but not a word to him. She moved her food around on her plate, but little made it to her mouth. The one time he dared to touch her, she shifted her hand away and asked the woman sitting next to her a question.

He would make this up to her somehow.

Not soon enough, Dr. Molasky stepped behind the podium and started the awards portion of the night. The recipients in other disciplines were called to the stage before it was his and Lily's turns. His name was called first.

Max accepted his award and said a few words of thanks. As he returned to his seat, Lily stood to go get hers. He congratulated her and briefly squeezed her hand as they moved past each other. She returned a tight smile. With shoulders squared, she stepped to the podium and thanked her staff, Dr. Lee and her lab employees. She accepted none of the praise and gave it all to those around her. How like Lily.

When she returned to the table, he stood and held her chair. She fingered her award as the next person's name was called. After that winner returned to their seat, Lily stood and said, "Excuse me."

Lily hadn't returned by the time the last award had been given. With those done, his father took the stage and said all the right things, then made his announcement.

Still there was no Lily.

Max didn't waste any time explaining anything to his parents. He exited the ballroom and headed straight for the restrooms. A woman assured him Lily wasn't there. His gut told him she'd left. Ordering his car brought around, he headed straight to Lily's house. He should have known when she excused herself, she wouldn't be back.

There were no lights on in the house when he pulled into her driveway. Her car was there, so she was, as well. He had to talk to her. Tonight. The next morning, he was headed back to New York. He'd promised to fill in for another doctor the next week. Those plans, he had to honor.

But leaving before talking to Lily wasn't possible either. He had to explain.

Max pushed the doorbell. For the third time. Still no lights. No sound of feet. Nothing.

Could she really be that stubborn? Of course she could. Hadn't she stayed away from conferences because she couldn't face him?

He huffed and started around the house to her bedroom window. Now he was acting like a stalker. Like a desperate man. He rapped his knuckles on the window. Still nothing. He tapped again.

Finally, the shadow of Lily appeared in the window. "What're you doing?"

"I'm trying to talk to you. Let me in."

"Go away."

She wasn't making it easy on him. Not that he had expected her to. "Lily, we need to talk."

Lily pointed toward the front. She had him wait on the porch long enough he feared she wouldn't open the door. Relief washed through him at the sound of the lock being released.

Lily didn't bother to turn the lights on. Not even a small welcome.

With the only glow coming from a distant streetlamp, he could still see she'd been crying. A lot.

He'd been the cause of those tears. He'd promised Ivy he wouldn't make Lily cry. His promises, he took pride in keeping. This time he'd failed. Somehow, he had to fix this. "Lily, I know you're upset, but I need to explain. Can I come in? Please."

She looked around him as if concerned about her neighbors. Her lips formed a tight line as she pushed the door wider and stepped back.

It wasn't an enthusiastic welcome, but he would take it. He entered and closed the door behind them. "It didn't happen the way you think it did."

Lily stood, her arms crossed over a knit tank top and shorts that showed the full length of her legs. Everything about her stance screaming "closed." "I'm not thinking anything."

He knew better than that. Lily was always thinking. "Do you mind if we turn on a light, sit down and talk like two rational adults?"

Lily growled, "That might be possible if I was feeling like a rational adult."

Max reached for her. She backed away. "Please, can we just sit down and talk this out?"

He couldn't remember another time in his life, except for when he'd asked his father to listen to him when Max said he was going into medicine, that he'd pleaded with someone to hear him out. He'd certainly never begged a woman he was interested in to give him a chance. Truthfully, he'd never had to or wanted to. So why did it matter so badly that Lily did?

Because he loved her.

"Okay. Have it your way. We'll do this standing and in the dark. I'm sorry you feel like you've been betrayed. My father did ask me to talk to you about packaging the products. He's always wanted me to go into the company and I saw this as something I could do for him that would help his business. I thought he might finally accept I went into medicine instead of his company. That I could offer something to his life's work. I guess what it comes down to is for once I wanted him to be proud of me. I hate that I even have to say that.

"I'm a grown man in a profession where I save lives and I'm good at my job, but I still need my father's acceptance. Medicine was never good enough for him, and this was one time I thought I could mesh the two. You got caught in the middle. I hadn't intended for that to happen."

Lily glared but still said nothing.

"I know you think I used you, betrayed you, especially after my Dad's insistence on announcing that his company would be packaging Vseal and Skintec together. It especially looked bad since you had only agreed this afternoon."

Lily put her hands on her hips and leaned toward him. "You mean to tell me that you didn't call and tell him of our agreement the second you left my house?"

"I didn't."

"Then, you must have been pretty sure of yourself or your father was of your abilities to seduce me into agreeing," she spat. "Did your father tell you to do anything you could to make it happen? Even take me to bed!"

"Hell, no! You make it sound like he's my pimp. Do you think I only made love to you because I wanted to get you to agree to a deal? That doesn't flatter me and it certainly degrades you."

"Well, what should I think?"

"Has it ever occurred to you that maybe I care about you? That I love you?" Saying the words out loud were a shock to him, but he realized he didn't care. They were true.

"You have a funny way of showing it!" Lily retorted.

"Or maybe you don't let anybody in enough to recognize it. You stay all tied up in your little shell, worried that you might not be in control of your world. You can't let go enough to let them show you love. Even with Ivy, you hold on so tightly it gives you an excuse not to take a chance or have some adventure."

"How dare you?" She took a step toward him, her eyes snapping. "The Casanova of the liver transplant world is telling me what it's like to really care about somebody. It's laughable. The best I can tell, you've spent your adult years caring only about yourself. The minute you have an opportunity to have a woman in your life who cares about you, the real you, the giving, caring you, you do nothing but use her. Now, I'm done here."

"How like you. Every time something goes wrong or it gets hard, you run off. Just like tonight. You just up and disappeared when you thought you might have to face conflict. You quit going to conferences because you didn't want to face you might be less than perfect. I'm not letting you hide this time."

"I'm not hiding from anything!"

A dry chuckle came from Max. "You've lived in Miami your entire life and have never been to the Everglades. You work all the time, and you never go to the Cuban area when you love the place. From what I can tell, you don't even have a hobby. You hold on to that image of the lonely girl with the mentally challenged sister like it's a lifeline. Ivy lives in a wonderful place where she's protected and taken care of and, most of all, happy. She has a full life, yet you still live behind the protective wall you built."

Lily glared at him. "She's like a child."

"In many ways, you've even held her back. She can do more than you let her do. If you let go some, she might surprise you. The only problem you'll have is how to fill the void with something. And that scares you. You cared for your patients. You take care of your sister. But what do you do for you?"

She staggered backward until she hit a table. Her hand gripped the edge. "I guess you got what you wanted. You made your father proud."

He said softly, "That might be what I thought I wanted. But not anymore. I want you."

She huffed. "You've made that clear. You want me so I'll sign on the dotted line in a business proposition. You're going to get what you want. I'll honor what I said. You send me the papers and I'll have my lawyer look at them. You can make your father proud then. Your job is done here."

"Lily, you don't have to agree." Could she make him feel angrier or more horrible?

"I said I'd do it, and your father made the announcement. I wouldn't dare pull out now. What would that do to his reputation and mine?"

Max took a step toward her. "See? There you go, not standing up for what you want."

She shook her head and put up a hand. "Why're you arguing with me when you got what you came after?"

"I'm going to say this one more time. It wasn't like that. All my father requested me to do was ask you. I did not pursue you with that in mind."

She crossed her arms again. "If I remember correctly, I was asked more than once."

The discussion had moved in a circle. Lily walked to the door and opened it. "You've told your side. I've said and heard all I want to. If you have anything else to say to me, make it through your daddy's company and my lawyer. You need to go."

Max stepped out on the porch. "Lily—"

She closed the door firmly between them.

CHAPTER TEN

LILY SLEEPWALKED THROUGH the next week. The only time Max wasn't at the forefront of her thoughts was when she was in surgery or seeing a patient. All she had done was go through the motions. How did a heart as broken as hers keep beating?

She made every effort to keep her life as normal and on track as possible. Those things she could handle. Could react and act as if everything in her world remained the same. Nighttime brought on its own set of problems. She crawled into bed as soon as she got home. When she was busy, she could breathe, but when she entered her bedroom, she missed Max with a power that had become physical. She of people thought being lovesick was a myth. After she'd closed the door on Max, she soon found out differently. She wrapped her arms tightly around herself and pulled her legs up until she formed a ball. Still, she couldn't keep the pain at bay.

Why, oh why had she let him into her life? Her bedroom? The pain of losing Max far surpassed the hurt of Jeff dumping her. It was so intense it consumed her. Life had become a hollow shell of what it once was. Those blissful days of Max were but a blur. She feared she'd never truly be happy again.

She didn't want to think about Max anymore. Yet she wanted to hear his voice, touch his face, kiss him...

His calls and texts pulled at her. The temptation to give in and respond was a constant shadow over her. If she did, what would change? It would just make the separation more painful. Leaving things as they were was the only way for her to survive. If what she was doing could be called that.

In an effort to keep her world as normal as possible, she picked up Ivy to come over to spend the night on Friday.

"Where is Max?" Ivy looked around the room.

"He had to go home. He doesn't live here. He lives in New York."

The expression on Ivy's face turned sad. "He was my friend."

"I know, honey. He is still your friend. You

just won't see him every often." *Or ever*, Lily left off.

"Is he coming back?"

"No, honey, I don't think he is." Lily worked to keep the wobble out of her voice.

Ivy placed her hand on Lily's arm. "He made you cry?"

"No, I'm fine." Ivy became a misty blur.

Ivy continued to watch Lily. "You do not think that I see and understand, but I do."

Lily's shocked gaze met hers.

"You are crying. Max promised not to make you cry."

"Sometimes people can't help what they do." Max could have, but Lily wouldn't let Ivy believe anything but good about him. He'd been wonderful to Ivy, and Lily wouldn't take that away from either one of them.

"Do you like Max?"

"I did." No matter how he had hurt her, Lily still loved him.

"You can like him again."

Lily turned her back to Ivy so she wouldn't see the tears come to her eyes. "I don't think that's going to happen."

"Did you have a fight?"

"Yes, honey, we had a fight and he had to go home."

Ivy moved around Lily to stare at her face.

"But you still cry. I am mad at him too. He promised."

Lily gave her a hug. "Thank you. I'm glad I have you for a sister. Now, let's talk about something else."

"But I miss my friend."

Lily needed to redirect Ivy to another subject. "What would you like to do tomorrow?"

"I want to learn to skate. A girl at the beach skated. Max told me I should learn."

Max would have. "Is that really what you want to do?"

Ivy nodded. "I want to try. Max said it's okay to fail. It's the not trying that's wrong."

Wasn't that what Max had been saying to her but in different words? Why hadn't she noticed that Ivy was more adventurous than her? Had she been hiding in a box she controlled, so she'd feel no pain from failure? "Okay, then we'll try. I've never done that before. It's time we learned."

Ivy nodded with enthusiasm.

Had she prevented Ivy from experiencing all she could because Lily had such tight guardrails around Ivy? At least Ivy was willing to try. Lily had pulled into a parking spot and stayed there until Max had come along. She'd become so regimented in her life she couldn't move. Afraid of being hurt. She couldn't trust anyone.

Max had proven he was a good guy. That he cared. He didn't need to go get Ivy, show her attention, do things she would enjoy. In surgery, in an emergency, Max had been supportive and helpful. He'd shown her tender care in and out of the bedroom. So why had she doubted him when he explained what had happened with his father? Had he really deserved the treatment she'd given him?

It was time she broadened her horizons. She'd been so caught up in her narrow life it was time to shake it up. She'd give up this morose existence she'd been living in and start making some changes. It was time she approached the world with a sense of wonder. "Ivy, is there anything else you'd like to learn to do?"

"I want to ride a bike. My friend knows how to. He rides around all the time. I could ride with him."

"I'd like to do that too. When you learn, we could bike down by the beach."

"Could we?" Ivy's excitement was infectious.

"Sure. You have been wanting to work off the compound. Do you still want to do that?"

"You mean at the shoe store?"

"Yes, I believe that's the place." It would take more fortitude for Lily to let her do it than Ivy would need to do the work. Facing fear was difficult.

Ivy nodded deeply. "I want to work at the shoe store."

"Okay. I'll talk to the director on Monday about you getting hired there." Lily's look turned stern. "But you have to promise me you won't ever run away again."

"I promise." Ivy gave her a long look. "You are different, Lily."

She felt changed but was surprised Ivy noticed. "How's that?"

"You were happy when Max was here. You are sad now, but you will be happy again."

"Yes, I will be." Lily said with more confidence than she'd felt in a week. She hugged Ivy. "We'll both be happy."

Max shifted in an uncomfortable leather chair in the reception area outside his father's office. What he needed to discuss with his parent was business, so he'd made an appointment instead of talking to him at home. His father had always listened marginally better at his office to anything Max had to say. For once, Max wanted a man-to-man discussion, not a father-to-son one. Max would be saying things the man wouldn't want to hear. Difficult things for Max to say and even more so for his father to listen to.

When Max left on Sunday morning to return to New York City, he'd thought about driving by Lily's house first. But then he really would've looked like a stalker. Instead, he decided to give her a few days to calm down, and then he would try to contact her.

He hadn't done anything wrong, but what he hated was it didn't look that way to Lily. Her past experiences made her believe she couldn't trust a man. Her ex had certainly let her down when he'd tried to use her. Max's stomach roiled. To Lily, it looked as if he'd done the same thing. Max had to make sure Lily understood he hadn't taken their relationship to a personal level because he wanted to get her to agree to the packaging.

He'd called daily after he'd left Miami. All he could do was leave a voicemail message, but Lily never returned any of them. He tried texting, but there was silence from Lily. Just as she had done before, Lily had gone into hiding. When he finished his business with his father, Max was headed back to Miami. He had to make things right between him and Lily. He couldn't accept less. If he'd learned anything in the last miserable week, it was that he needed Lily to make his life complete.

His father's assistant said, "You may go in now."

Max pulled the modern floor-to-ceiling door open and stepped into the spacious glass-and-wood space. It was much like his father: sleek, clean and minimal. His father sat behind a large desk in the center of the room.

Shock rocked through Max when his father stood and hurried around his desk. Instead of offering his hand, he hugged Max.

"Come in. Come in. You did a great job getting that doctor to agree to the packaging."

Everything his father said went against Max's grain. Max's body tensed. He pushed away. "Her name is Dr. Lily Evans. Lily."

His father didn't miss a beat. "Yes, yes, Dr. Evans. You did it."

"Yeah, I did it," Max mumbled. But he wasn't proud of how it had all panned out. Lily felt used and that's the last thing he wanted to have happen. He'd lost more than one night's sleep because of it. It didn't help that he missed having her in his arms.

"Your mom is glad to have you home," his father continued as if he didn't recognize Max's lack of enthusiasm, which Max was sure he didn't. "Tell me what's so important that you felt the need to come all the way to Chicago to talk to me so late on a Friday evening."

His father returned to his seat behind the desk, and Max took a chair in front of him.

Max inhaled deeply and let his breath out slowly. This is the moment he'd been preparing for since he'd made the decision days earlier. "We need to get a few things straight."

His father's brows rose. "In regard to…?"

"Mine and Lily's merger. I have some stipulations I want to include in the contract."

His father's look turned to stone. He placed his hands across his chest in a defensive manner. "Such as?"

"The first is you will agree to a ten-year proprietary ownership period instead of the usual twenty years."

His father's chair creaked when he sat forward so quickly.

Max didn't pause. "I'd also like for my share of the profits to be designated to go to the Palm Plantation in Miami along with one third of the company profits directed to go to the Liver Foundation."

"I don't think I—"

Max pushed on. "That's how it has to be if I'm going to sign the contract. Otherwise, I'll take Vseal elsewhere."

His father stood. "You'd do that to my company?"

"I don't think I'm doing anything to your company. You'll have the prestige of being the one to put the package out. And the income. That should lead to more business for you."

"Why're you doing this?" Disbelief covered his father's face.

Max shrugged. "It's the right thing to do."

His father sat again. "Mmm, I think there's more to it than that. You're doing it for that doctor. You fell for her."

Max's jaw tightened. His father remained so focused on his work he still made no effort to remember Lily's name. Even when he'd been reminded a number of times.

"I'm in love with Lily." Max emphasized Lily's name.

"Is that so?"

"Yes, it is. What I did to her was unforgivable." Max intended to make her understand he couldn't live without her.

"What did you do? I thought all you did was ask her to let us package your products together." There was more interest in his father's voice than expected.

"I did, but you made the announcement after she'd just told me she would agree. Lily feels she has been manipulated."

His father huffed. "How do you manipulate someone into making millions?"

"Lily is more interested in helping people than she is in the money."

His father's look of disbelief was typical. "What do you mean? We develop our products to make money and increase business."

Max moved to the edge of his seat as if preparing to leave. "In that case, maybe Lily and I need to take our products elsewhere."

His father waved his hand. "I don't want you to do that."

"Then you agree to my stipulations?" Max fixed his look on his father daring him not to approve.

"You aren't leaving the company much of a profit margin, or you either."

Max shrugged. "Lily has a mentally challenged sister who lives at Palm Plantation. I want there to be constant funds for the upkeep of the place for Ivy and the other residents, with or without the ability to pay."

"Is that all?" His father voice was a cross between frustration and admiration.

"That's all for me. Lily may have more demands when the time comes. I don't know."

"You're not giving me a choice, are you?"

Max shook his head.

His father watched Max over the top of his hands. "What's all of this about?"

"This is about me trying to make up for a wrong. I got so wrapped up in trying to prove myself to you that I hurt someone I care about."

"Trying to prove something to me?" His father's voice went higher with surprise. "What do you mean? You don't have to prove anything to me."

"I know you weren't pleased with me when I went into medicine instead of joining the company. When you came to me and asked about talking to Lily, I thought if I got the packaging contract, then it might make it up to you. Instead, I hurt Lily with my selfishness." Disgust welled in his gut.

"I didn't ask you to hurt her. I thought you might know her. I just thought it was a logical step to ask you to contact her."

"I know that. I'm the one who let it get out of hand." He met his father's gaze. "Just as I've let other things go on too long. I should have said this long ago. I love you, Dad. I do. I'm sorry I disappointed you by not wanting to work at The James Company, but I'm good at my profession. I save lives. I'm well respected for my abilities. It's time for me to stop being that kid who's always trying to please his father. Those days are gone. I hope you can accept my life decisions, but if not, that's for you to deal with."

"Of course, I hoped you'd want to work in my company, but I never said I wasn't proud of you."

"No, but you've made it clear in every way possible. In fact, you even implied that if I didn't approach Lily about contracting with you, then I might be the cause of your company having financial trouble."

"I think you misunderstood."

Max sat straighter in his chair. "No, Dad, I did not."

His father waved a hand as if what Max said meant nothing. "All I've ever wanted was to share my business with my son. But that doesn't mean that I'm not proud of you. Of course I've heard of your good work. You do save lives. I recognize the importance of that. I may not have said it in the past, but I am proud of you."

Max's breath caught. He'd just heard something he'd never heard before.

"Who wouldn't be proud of that glue you developed? I was confident you were a chip off the old block. I do have to admit I hoped you'd give up practicing medicine and start working on medical developments for me. But I quickly figured out that wasn't going to happen."

"No, it isn't," Max said in a firm voice.

"I'm a businessman, Max. You've always known that. I see the bottom line."

"Yeah, Dad, that's the one sure thing about you." Something Max couldn't always agree with.

"That doesn't mean I'm not proud of you. I didn't want to, but I admired how you stood up to me and found your own path."

"You did?" Max had no doubt his shock rang out clearly. "Thanks for that. It means a lot."

His father came around the desk as Max stood. The older man took Max into a hug that Max returned. "I'll make your demands work somehow. Are you going after… Lily?"

His father had used Lily's name correctly for the first time. "I am. As soon as I leave here, I'm headed to Miami. I hope I can convince her that I want whatever she wants."

"Then, start by blaming it on me." His father grinned.

Max chuckled. "I'll do that, but I do have to put some responsibility on myself."

"The one thing I've learned with your mother is that eating humble pie can go a long way toward easing the problem."

Max and his father had rarely shared this type of interaction. It felt good. "Thanks, Dad, I'll keep that in mind."

"Your mother said she thought Lily might be that special one by the way you looked at her."

Max smiled. "Mom would notice."

"Yeah. She also reminded me that I'm a father first and a businessman second. And for me to keep that in mind when dealing with you. Forgive me if sometimes I forget that."

"Already done. I love you, Dad."

His father looked a little taken back, but he responded, "I love you too."

Ten days had gone by. Lily had counted every one. It was the same amount of time Max had been in town. The last had been far more painful than those before them. They seemed like years instead of days.

Despite her disappointment in Max, she'd taken some of what Max had said to heart and had already started making some changes in her life. She'd set work hours, and she stuck to them, not lingering at the hospital because she had no other place to go. She used the time she gained to join a yoga class, where she had started meeting people who had nothing to do with the medical field. One evening she spent in a chair in her backyard beneath a banana tree, reading a book just for fun.

Max might've broken her heart, but he'd

made her take off the mask she'd worn and face her need to move forward. She planned to do something new every month, even if it was just walking around a part of her neighborhood she'd never been to before. She shouldn't have been, but she was surprised how much adding something new and simple affected her world. Like the pop of a champagne bottle, her life had been released to flow freely and bubble.

The only problem was she had no one to share her newfound life with. As much as she enjoyed it, she still missed Max with every fiber of her being. She dreamed of him each night and reached for him every morning. All those beautiful memories she'd thought she'd have they were there but didn't hold her and nestle her against a warm body.

The second Tuesday afternoon after Max had left, a large envelope was delivered to her office. The James Company logo in the corner gave away who it was from. It would be the contract papers she'd been expecting. The ones that would tie her and Max together forever and not in the way she wanted.

Lily opened the package. On top of all the legal papers lay a note with Mr. James's letterhead on it.

Dr. Evans,

It was a pleasure to meet you. I think that you will find you will like working with The James Company.

I have enclosed the contract and particulars that will cement our relationship. As you read through, you will see some out-of-the-ordinary stipulations. Max would not agree to his part without them.

Please contact me if you have any questions.

Later that evening, Lily pulled one leg up beneath her as she settled on the cushion in the chair in her backyard. She opened the book she'd been reading. Over the last few hours, she'd thought of nothing but the odd but pleasantly surprising demands in the contract from The James Company. She would let her lawyer review it, but she had already decided to sign it. Max had once again taken care of her and Ivy.

Lily had already figured out she'd been wrong about him and the contract confirmed it. She wished her happily-ever-after could be that easily achieved. Would Max forgive her for thinking the worst of him? The longer time went on, the harder it would be to face Max, but she was going to have to. Tomorrow, she would call him. By then, she would have her nerve up.

What he'd said about her hiding kept running through her mind. Wasn't that what she was doing again? That, too, had to stop. She wouldn't wait to call him tomorrow. She would do it tonight. Thank him. Apologize. She needed to do it right away. Ivy asked about Max every time they were together. Maybe by Friday night when she came to stay, Lily could give Ivy an update on Max.

Lily opened the book. She'd read a while, fix a salad and then make the call. It was time to face her mistakes.

The sound of a car door closing reached her ears, but she didn't give it much thought. It was the time of day most of her neighbors were coming home for the evening. It wasn't until she sensed someone watching her that she looked up.

She gasped. Her heart raced as her book fluttered to the ground. *Max.*

He stood at the corner of her house.

Lily tried to move but couldn't. All she could do was stare.

"I tried the doorbell." He sounded unsure.

The confident, charming and always-quick-with-a-humorous-quip Max James acted as if he didn't know what to say or do next. She shouldn't have been surprised after their last meeting. Hadn't she slammed the door between them? Worse, not taken his calls or answered his texts. The amazing part was that he'd even bothered to come see her. "Max, what are you doing here?"

"Uh, may I join you?" He shifted his feet.

Was he nervous? "Sure." She straightened and indicated the other chair beside her, her hand shaking. Her heart fluttered. Max was actually here.

Lily feasted her eyes on him as he strolled toward her, soaking in his every detail. He looked ruggedly handsome with a five o'clock shadow covering his jaw. His dark hair had grown, and a lock hung over his forehead. He wore a floral shirt with a brightly colored birds-of-paradise pattern, and tan cargo shorts. Brown sandals protected his feet. He was all she'd ever wanted and more.

"It's good to see you, Lily." He took the chair next to her.

"Max, I—"

"No, Lily. I need to go first." He took a deep breath. "I came to tell you how sorry I am. I promise I didn't spend time with you, make love to you or have something to do with Ivy just to get your agreement. I told my father I wasn't participating in any more of his deals.

In fact, I told him a number of things I should have said long ago. I hurt you, and I don't want to ever do that again."

"It was my fault—"

He put up a hand. "Let me finish. You should have received the contract. Sign it or don't, that is up to you. I want you to be pleased with it. That's all I ever want is for you to be happy."

Her eyes narrowed. "Did you come all this way just to tell me that?"

Max shrugged. "That and other things. But they can wait until we work the business out." He paused. "I didn't mean for things to happen the way they did."

"I know."

His eyes widened. "You do?"

"Yeah. I figured it out not long after you left. But I couldn't bring myself to tell you that. I've been putting my issues with Jeff, or really my lifelong issues of having control, making sure Ivy wasn't hurt and me, as well, off on you. You were right. I keep a protective wall around me. But somehow, you climbed over it. It has taken me years, but because of you, I now know that to have happiness, sometimes you must accept the pain of loss. I can't protect Ivy all the time, or myself either.

"I've made assumptions about you based on hearsay and that wasn't fair to you. Over and over, you have proven to be a stand-up guy, one I could depend on. I couldn't have asked someone to be nicer to Ivy than you have been."

"I like Ivy. I've enjoyed getting to know her."

"I know that. I knew it last week. I'm sorry about how I treated you. I was just scared."

"Of me?" Max looked horrified.

"Yes, no. Of my feelings. About how much you mattered to me."

Max's stance eased.

Lily went on, fearing she might not get it all out if she didn't. "But we live so far apart. How can we ever have a real relationship when we're in different parts of the country? It would just end one day anyway. I didn't want it to hurt any more than it already did to have you leave. I was planning to call you tonight and tell you all this, and you showed up. I really am sorry I didn't trust you. You didn't deserve that. The stipulations you put in the contract prove that."

Max took her hand. "We both messed up. Do you think we can start over?"

"Yeah," she nodded. "I would like that."

"Friends?"

Lily was hoping for more, but she'd take that over nothing. Her hands tightened on his. "Friends."

"I like the sound of that," he said thoughtfully. "It has a nice ring to it. I'm not known for having women friends. Casual relationships, yes, but I don't want those anymore and especially not with you." He gave her a sheepish look. "You've changed me, Lily Evans. For the better."

She had?

"I'm crazy about you, Lily. You have shown me what I want out of life. You make my days easy and my nights amazing. I know what acceptance is because of you. I want to have you with me forever. I want to help you see about Ivy and be the brother she has never had. I want—I need—you always. I love you more than I can say."

Lily's eyes swam with moisture, blurring the wonderful man in front of her. These were tears of happiness instead of pain. She rose and threw herself into Max's arms.

"Whoa, that must mean you feel the same."

She kissed his neck, his cheek before her lips found his. "You bet I do."

Max gathered her to him, pulling her legs to the side so that she sat across his lap. Lily continued to kiss him, running her fingers through his hair. His hand slid over her back and up to slip under her hair. He took the kiss deeper, making her moan with delight. She'd missed him so much. Having Max's kisses again was like finding home.

He pulled back but continued to hold her close. She looked into his beautiful blue eyes. He wiped the moisture from her cheeks. "You need to stop crying. I promised Ivy I wouldn't make you cry."

"These are good tears. Tears of happiness. I've missed you so much."

"Honey, I've missed you too." Max kissed her tenderly.

She pulled away. "I need to tell you something."

"What's that?"

"I love you."

"I love you, too, with everything in me. I know this has all happened pretty fast, but I have something else I want to discuss with you." His lips brushed her cheek. "Dr. Lee offered me a position in your department. What would you think about me moving to Miami?"

Lily's mouth fell open. "You are relocating here?"

"Only if it's okay with you. I don't want to do anything that you don't agree with."

"Of course I agree with it. I can't think of anything more perfect." Lily wrapped her arms around his neck and kissed him soundly. Max eagerly returned her embrace. She pulled back.

"I need to warn you that I've started making some changes in my life."

"You have? I hope they don't exclude me."

She grinned. "Never. I agreed to let Ivy start working at a shoe store off the compound. She's only been there a couple of days but loves it. From what I can tell, the owner is pleased, as well. She and I learned to roller-skate the other Saturday. She wants to learn to ride a bike."

"That's great."

"I've started keeping regular hours at the hospital and—" she reached for the book and placed it on the arm of the chair, "—I'm taking time to read a book."

"You are making some changes. I'm proud of you. I'll try to add to your fun when I can." His hand slid along her bare leg as he gave her a wicked grin. "My plans are to move down here as soon as I can, date you for a while, maybe move in if invited, then I'm going to ask Ivy if I have permission to marry you. Then I want to give you that baby you want."

Lily's gaze met his. "Do you mind if I tweak the plan just a little?"

Max's eyes filled with concern. Was he still worried she'd not forgiven him? "I think the moving here as soon as possible sounds great, but I think you should move in here when you come. As for marrying you, I'm ready for that whenever you are. As for having your baby, I can't think of anything that would give me more joy."

His look had brightened as she spoke. "Me, either, except for maybe having two."

"At the same time?" she squeaked.

Max shrugged. "Twins or singles—I just want to make a family with you. And for Ivy to be an aunt."

"It sounds like a life I won't run from."

He kissed her tenderly. "If you do, I'll come find you."

Lily kissed him deeply. "You are all I'll ever need. You are more than enough."

Max looked into her eyes a moment as if he were taking in her words and holding them close. "Thank you for saying that." His hand slipped under her shorts to cup her butt cheek. "Do you mind if we get started on that baby right away? I have missed you. And I want to show you how much I love you."

Lily stood and Max followed. She went up on her toes and kissed him. "I love you."

"And I love you. With you, I am whole."

* * * * *

If you enjoyed this story, check out these other great reads from Susan Carlisle

Taming the Hot-Shot Doc
Reunited with Her Daredevil Doc
The Single Dad's Holiday Wish
Pacific Paradise, Second Chance

All available now!